AVESTA: Vendidad

Translated by James Darmesteter

AVESTA: Vendidad

Table of Contents

AVESTA: Vendidad..1
    Translated by James Darmesteter..1
    FARGARD 1. Sixteen perfect lands created by Ahura Mazda, and as many plagues created by Angra Mainyu..1
    FARGARD 2. Myths of Yima...4
    FARGARD 3. The Earth...11
    FARGARD 4. Contracts and offenses...18
    FARGARD 5. Purity laws...28
    FARGARD 6. Purity laws...38
    FARGARD 7. Purity laws...45
    FARGARD 8. Purity laws...56
    FARGARD 9. The Nine Nights' Barashnum..75
    FARGARD 10. Formulas recited during the process of cleansing.....86
    FARGARD 11. Special formulas for cleansing several objects...........90
    FARGARD 12. The Upaman: how long it lasts for different relatives....94
    FARGARD 13. The Dog...99
    FARGARD 14. Atoning for the murder of a water–dog......................110
    FARGARD 15. Regarding certain sins and obligations.......................113
    FARGARD 16. Purity laws regarding menstruation............................120
    FARGARD 17. Hair and nails...124
    FARGARD 18...125
    FARGARD 19...136
    FARGARD 20. Thrita, the First Healer..145
    FARGARD 21...148
    FARGARD 22. Angra Mainyu creates 99,999 diseases; Ahura Mazda counters with the Holy Manthra and with Airyaman.........................152

AVESTA: Vendidad

Translated by James Darmesteter

Kessinger Publishing reprints thousands of hard-to-find books!

Visit us at http://www.kessinger.net

FARGARD 1. Sixteen perfect lands created by Ahura Mazda, and as many plagues created by Angra Mainyu.

1.
Ahura Mazda spake unto Spitama Zarathushtra, saying: I have made every land dear (to its people), even though it had no charms whatever in it: had I not made every land dear (to its people), even though it had no charms whatever in it, then the whole living world would have invaded the Airyana Vaeja.
2.
[Clause 2 in the Vendidad Sada is composed of Zend quotations in the Commentary that illustrate the alternative process of creation: 'First, Ahura Mazda would create a land of such kind that its dwellers might like it, and there could be nothing more delightful. Then he who is all death would bring against it a counter-creation.']

The first of the good lands and countries which I, Ahura Mazda, created, was the Airyana Vaeja, by the Vanguhi Daitya.
Thereupon came Angra Mainyu, who is all death, and he counter-created the serpent in the river and Winter, a work of the Daevas.
3.
There are ten winter months there, two summer months; and those are cold for the waters, cold for the earth, cold for the

AVESTA: Vendidad

trees. Winter falls there, the worst of all plagues.
4.
The second of the good lands and countries which I, Ahura Mazda, created, was the plain [Doubtful] which the Sughdhas inhabit.

Thereupon came Angra Mainyu, who is all death, and he counter-created the locust, which brings death unto cattle and plants.
5.
The third of the good lands and countries which I, Ahura Mazda, created, was the strong, holy Mouru.
Thereupon came Angra Mainyu, who is all death, and he counter-created plunder and sin [Doubtful].
6.
The fourth of the good lands and countries which I, Ahura Mazda, created, was the beautiful Bakhdhi with high-lifted banner.

Thereupon came Angra Mainyu, who is all death, and he counter-created the ants and the ant-hills.
7.
The fifth of the good lands and countries which I, Ahura Mazda, created, was Nisaya, that lies between the Mouru and Bakhdhi.

Thereupon came Angra Mainyu, who is all death, and he counter-created the sin of unbelief.
8.
The sixth of the good lands and countries which I, Ahura Mazda, created, was the house-deserting Haroyu
Thereupon came Angra Mainyu, who is all death, and he counter-created tears and wailing.
9.
The seventh of the good lands and countries which I, Ahura Mazda, created, was Vaekereta, of the evil shadows.
Thereupon came Angra Mainyu, who is all death, and he counter-created the Pairika Knathaiti, who claves unto Keresaspa.
10.
The eighth of the good lands and countries which I, Ahura

AVESTA: Vendidad

Mazda, created, was Urva of the rich pastures.
Thereupon came Angra Mainyu, who is all death, and he counter-created the sin of pride.

11.
The ninth of the good lands and countries which I, Ahura Mazda, created, was Khnenta which the Vehrkanas inhabit.
Thereupon came Angra Mainyu, who is all death, and he counter-created a sin for which there is no atonement, the unnatural sin.

12.
The tenth of the good lands and countries which I, Ahura Mazda, created, was the beautiful Harahvaiti.
Thereupon came Angra Mainyu, who is all death, and he counter-created a sin for which there is no atonement, the burying of the dead.

13.
The eleventh of the good lands and countries which I, Ahura Mazda, created, was the bright, glorious Haetumant.
Thereupon came Angra Mainyu, who is all death, and he counter-created the evil work of witchcraft.

14.
And this is the sign by which it is known, this is that by which it is seen at once: wheresoever they may go and raise a cry of sorcery, there the worst works of witchcraft go forth. From there they come to kill and strike at heart, and they bring locusts as many as they want.

15.
The twelfth of the good lands and countries which I, Ahura Mazda, created, was Ragha of the three races.
Thereupon came Angra Mainyu, who is all death, and he counter-created the sin of utter unbelief.

16.
The thirteenth of the good lands and countries which I, Ahura Mazda, created, was the strong, holy Chakhra.
Thereupon came Angra Mainyu, who is all death, and he counter-created a sin for which there is no atonement, the cooking of corpses.

17.
The fourteenth of the good lands and countries which I, Ahura

AVESTA: Vendidad

Mazda, created, was the four-cornered Varena, for which was born
Thraetaona, who smote Azi Dahaka.
Thereupon came Angra Mainyu, who is all death, and he counter-created
abnormal issues in women, and barbarian oppression.
18.
The fifteenth of the good lands and countries which I, Ahura
Mazda, created, was the Seven Rivers.
Thereupon came Angra Mainyu, who is all death, and he counter-created
abnormal issues in women, and excessive heat.
19.
The sixteenth of the good lands and countries which I, Ahura
Mazda, created, was the land by the sources (?) of the Rangha,
where people live who have no chiefs.
Thereupon came Angra Mainyu, who is all death, and he counter-created
Winter, a work of the Daevas.
20.
There are still other lands and countries, beautiful and deep,
longing and asking for the good, and bright.

FARGARD 2. Myths of Yima

1.
Zarathushtra asked Ahura Mazda: O Ahura Mazda, most beneficent
Spirit, Maker of the material world, thou Holy One! Who was the
first mortal, before myself, Zarathushtra, with whom thou, Ahura
Mazda, didst converse, whom thou didst teach the Religion of Ahura,
the Religion of Zarathushtra? 2. Ahura Mazda answered: The fair
Yima, the good shepherd, O holy Zarathushtra! he was the first
mortal, before thee, Zarathushtra, with whom I, Ahura Mazda, did
converse, whom I taught the Religion of Ahura, the Religion of
Zarathushtra. 3. Unto him, O Zarathushtra, I, Ahura Mazda, spake,
saying: 'Well, fair Yima, son of Vivanghat, be thou the preacher

AVESTA: Vendidad

and the bearer of my Religion!' And the fair Yima, O Zarathushtra, replied unto me, saying: 'I was not born, I was not taught to be the preacher and the bearer of thy Religion.'

4.

Then I, Ahura Mazda, said thus unto him, O Zarathushtra: 'Since thou dost not consent to be the preacher and the bearer of my Religion, then make thou my world increase, make my world grow: consent thou to nourish, to rule, and to watch over my world.'

5.

And the fair Yima replied unto me, O Zarathushtra, saying: 'Yes! I will make thy world increase, I will make thy world grow. Yes! I will nourish, and rule, and watch over thy world. There shall be, while I am king, neither cold wind not hot wind, neither disease nor death.'

6.

[] Vd2.6 is composed of unconnected Zend quotations, which are no part of the text and are introduced by the commentator for the purpose of showing that 'although Yima did not teach the law and train pupils, he was nevertheless a faithful and a holy man, and rendered men holy too (?).' See Fragments of the Vendidad.

Then I, Ahura Mazda, brought two implements unto him: a golden seal and a poniard inlaid with gold. Behold, here Yima bears the royal sway!

7.

[Obscure.]

8.

Thus, under the sway of Yima, three hundred winters passed away, and the earth was replenished with flocks and herds, with men and dogs and birds and with red blazing fires, and there was room no more for flocks, herds, and men.

9.

Then I warned the fair Yima, saying: 'O fair Yima, son of Vivanghat, the earth has become full of flocks and herds, of men and dogs and birds and of red blazing fires, and there is room no more for flocks, herds, and men.'

AVESTA: Vendidad

10.
Then Yima stepped forward, in light, southwards, on the way of the sun, and (afterwards) he pressed the earth with the golden seal, and bored it with the poniard, speaking thus: 'O Spenta Armaiti, kindly 'Do this out of kindness to the creatures' (Comm.) open asunder and stretch thyself afar, to bear flocks and herds and men.'

11.
And Yima made the earth grow larger by one-third than it was before, and there came flocks and herds and men, at their will and wish, as many as he wished.

12.
Thus, under the sway of Yima, six hundred winters passed away, and the earth was replenished with flocks and herds, with men and dogs and birds and with red blazing fires, and there was room no more for flocks, herds, and men.

13.
And I warned the fair Yima, saying: 'O fair Yima, son of Vivanghat, the earth has become full of flocks and herds, of men and dogs and birds and of red blazing fires, and there is room no more for flocks, herds, and men.'

14.
Then Yima stepped forward, in light, southwards, on the way of the sun, and (afterwards) he pressed the earth with the golden seal, and bored it with the poniard, speaking thus: 'O Spenta Armaiti, kindly) open asunder and stretch thyself afar, to bear flocks and herds and men.'

15.
And Yima made the earth grow larger by two-thirds than it was before, and there came flocks and herds and men, at their will and wish, as many as he wished.

16.
Thus, under the sway of Yima, nine hundred winters passed away, and the earth was replenished with flocks and herds, with men and dogs and birds and with red blazing fires, and there was room no more for flocks, herds, and men.

AVESTA: Vendidad

17.
And I warned the fair Yima, saying: 'O fair Yima, son of Vivanghat, the earth has become full of flocks and herds, of men and dogs and birds and of red blazing fires, and there is room no more for flocks, herds, and men.'

18.
Then Yima stepped forward, in light, southwards, on the way of the sun, and (afterwards) he pressed the earth with the golden seal, and bored it with the poniard, speaking thus: 'O Spenta Armaiti, kindly) open asunder and stretch thyself afar, to bear flocks and herds and men.'

19.
And Yima made the earth grow larger by two-thirds than it was before, and there came flocks and herds and men, at their will and wish, as many as he wished.

20.
The Maker, Ahura Mazda, called together a meeting of the celestial Yazatas in the Airyana Vaejo of high renown, by the Vanguhi Dairya.

The fair Yima, the good shepherd, called together a meeting of the best of the mortals, in the Airyana Vaejo of high renown, by the Vanguhi Daitya.

21.
To that meeting came Ahura Mazda, in the Airyana Vaejo of high renown, by the Vanguhi Daitya; he came together with the celestial Yazatas.

To that meeting came the fair Yima, the good shepherd, in the Airyana Vaejo of high renown, by the Vanguhi Daitya; he came together with the best of the mortals.

22.
And Ahura Mazda spake unto Yima, saying: 'O fair Yima, son of Vivanghat! Upon the material world the evil winters are about to fall, that shall bring the fierce, deadly frost; upon the material world the evil winters are about to fall, that shall make snow-flakes fall thick, even an aredvi deep on the highest tops of mountains 'Even where it (the snow) is least, it will be one Vitasti two fingers

AVESTA: Vendidad

deep' (Comm.); that is, fourteen fingers deep .
23.
'And the beasts that live in the wilderness The
Comm. has, strangely enough, 'for instance, Ispahan.',
and those that live on the tops of the mountains 'For
instance, Aparsen (the Upairisaena or Hindu-Kush).',
and those that live in the bosom of the dale 'For
instance, Khorastan (the plain of Khorasan).' shall
take shelter in underground abodes.
24.
'Before that winter, the country would bear plenty of grass
for cattle, before the waters had flooded it. Now after the melting
of the snow, O Yima, a place wherein the footprint of a sheep
may be seen will be a wonder in the world.
25.
'Therefore make thee a Vara, long as a riding-ground on every
side of the square 'Two hathras long on every side'
(Comm.) A hathra is about an English mile. , and
thither bring the seeds of sheep and oxen, of men, of dogs, of
birds, and of red blazing fires. Therefore make thee a Vara, long
as a riding-ground on every side of the square, to be an abode
for man; a Vara, long as a riding-ground on every side of the
square, for oxen and sheep.
26.
'There thou shalt make waters flow in a bed a hathra long;
there thou shalt settle birds, on the green that never fades,
with food that never fails. There thou shalt establish dwelling-places,
consisting of a house with a balcony, a courtyard, and as gallery The
last three words are of doubtful meaning. .
27.
'Thither thou shalt bring the seeds of men and women, of the
greatest, best, and finest on this earth; thither thou shalt bring
the seeds of every kind of cattle, of the greatest, best, and
finest on this earth.
28.
'Thither thou shalt bring the seeds of every kind of tree,

AVESTA: Vendidad

of the highest of size and sweetest of odor on this earth 'The
highest of size, like the cypress and the plane-tree; the sweetest
of odor, like the rose and the jessamine' (Comm.) ;
thither thou shalt bring the seeds of every kind of fruit, the
best of savor and sweetest of odor 'The best of savor,
like the date; the sweetest of odor, like the citron' (Comm.) .
All those seeds shalt thou bring, two of every kind, to be kept
inexhaustible there, so long as those men shall stay in the Vara.
29. 'There shall be no humpbacked, none bulged forward there;
no impotent, no lunatic; no malicious, no liar; no one spiteful,
none jealous; no one with decayed tooth, no leprous to be pent
up, nor any of the brands wherewith Angra Mainyu stamps the bodies
of mortals.
30.
'In the largest part of the place thou shalt make nine streets,
six in the middle part, three in the smallest. To the streets
of the largest part thou shalt bring a thousand seeds of men and
women; to the streets of the middle part, six hundred; to the
streets of the smallest part, three hundred. That Vara thou shalt
seal up with thy golden seal, and thou shalt make a door, and
a window self-shining within.'
31.
Then Yima said within himself: 'How shall I manage to make
that Vara which Ahura Mazda has commanded me to make?' And Ahura
Mazda said unto Yima: 'O fair Yima, son of Vivanghat! Crush the
earth with a stamp of thy heel, and then knead it with thy hands,
as the potter does when kneading the potter's clay.'
32.
[And Yima did as Ahura Mazda wished; he crushed the earth
with a stamp of his heel, he kneaded it with his hands, as the
potter does when kneading the potter's clay From the
Vendidad Sada. .]
33.
And Yima made a Vara, long as a riding-ground on every side
of the square. There he brought the seeds of sheep and oxen, of
men, of dogs, of birds, and of red blazing fires. He made a Vara,

AVESTA: Vendidad

long as a riding-ground on every side of the square, to be an abode for men; a Vara, long as a riding-ground on every side of the square, for oxen and sheep.

34.
There he made waters flow in a bed a hathra long; there he settled birds, on the green that never fades, with food that never fails. There he established dwelling-places, consisting of a house with a balcony, a courtyard, and a gallery.

35.
There he brought the seeds of men and women, of the greatest, best, and finest on this earth; there he brought the seeds of every kind of cattle, of the greatest, best, and finest on this earth.

36.
There he brought the seeds of every kind of tree, of the highest of size and sweetest of odor on this earth; there he brought the seeds of every kind of fruit, the best of savor and sweetest of odor. All those seeds he brought, two of every kind, to be kept inexhaustible there, so long as those men shall stay in the Vara.

37.
And there were no humpbacked, none bulged forward there; no impotent, no lunatic; no one malicious, no liar; no one spiteful, none jealous; no one with decayed tooth, no leprous to be pent up, nor any of the brands wherewith Angra Mainyu stamps the bodies of mortals.

38.
In the largest part of the place he made nine streets, six in the middle part, three in the smallest. To the streets of the largest part he brought a thousand seeds of men and women; to the streets of the middle part, six hundred; to the streets of the smallest part, three hundred. That Vara he sealed up with the golden ring, and he made a door, and a window self-shining within.

39.
O Maker of the material world, thou Holy One! What are the lights that give light in the Vara which Yima made?

AVESTA: Vendidad

40.
Ahura Mazda answered: 'There are uncreated lights and created lights The Commentary has here the following Avestan quotation: 'The uncreated light shines from above; all the created lights shine from below.' . The one thing missed there is the sight of the stars, the moon, and the sun, and a year seems only as a day.

41.
'Every fortieth year, to every couple two are born, a male and a female. And thus it is for every sort of cattle. And the men in the Vara which Yima made live the happiest life 'They live there for 150 years; some say, they never die' (Comm.) .'

42.
O Maker of the material world, thou Holy One! Who is he who brought the Religion of Mazda into the Vara which Yima made? Ahura Mazda answered: 'It was the bird Karshipta, O holy Zarathushtra!'

43.
O Maker of the material world, thou Holy One! Who are the Lord and the Master there? Ahura Mazda answered: 'Urvatat-nara, O Zarathushtra! and thyself, Zarathushtra.'

FARGARD 3. The Earth

1.
O Maker of the material world, thou Holy one! Which is the first place where the Earth feels most happy? Ahura Mazda answered: 'It is the place whereon one of the faithful steps forward, O Spitama Zarathushtra! with the log in his hand, the Baresma in his hand, the milk in his hand, the mortar in his hand, lifting up his voice in good accord with religion, and beseeching Mithra, the lord of the rolling country-side, and Rama Hvastra.'

2,3.

AVESTA: Vendidad

O Maker of the material world, thou Holy one! Which is the
second place where the Earth feels most happy? Ahura Mazda answered:
'It is the place whereon one of the faithful erects a house with
a priest within, with cattle, with a wife, with children, and
good herds within; and wherein afterwards the cattle continue
to thrive, virtue to thrive, fodder to thrive, the dog to thrive,
the wife to thrive, the child to thrive, the fire to thrive, and
every blessing of life to thrive.'

4.
O Maker of the material world, thou Holy one! Which is the
third place where the Earth feels most happy? Ahura Mazda answered:
'It is the place where one of the faithful sows most corn, grass,
and fruit, O Spitama Zarathushtra! where he waters ground that
is dry, or drains ground that is too wet.'

5.
O Maker of the material world, thou Holy one! Which is the
fourth place where the Earth feels most happy? Ahura Mazda answered:
'It is the place where there is most increase of flocks and herds.'

6.
O Maker of the material world, thou Holy one! Which is the
fifth place where the Earth feels most happy? Ahura Mazda answered:
'It is the place where flocks and herds yield most dung.'

7.
O Maker of the material world, thou Holy one! Which is the
first place where the Earth feels sorest grief? Ahura Mazda answered:
'It is the neck of Arezura, whereon the hosts of fiends rush forth
from the burrow of the Druj.'

8.
O Maker of the material world, thou Holy one! Which is the
second place where the Earth feels sorest grief? Ahura Mazda answered:
'It is the place wherein most corpses of dogs and of men lie buried.'

9.
O Maker of the material world, thou Holy one! Which is the
third place where the Earth feels sorest grief? Ahura Mazda answered:
'It is the place whereon stand most of those Dakhmas on which
the corpses of men are deposited.'

AVESTA: Vendidad

10.
O Maker of the material world, thou Holy one! Which is the fourth place where the Earth feels sorest grief? Ahura Mazda answered: 'It is the place wherein are most burrows of the creatures of Angra Mainyu 'Where there are most Khrafstras' (noxious animals). .

11.
O Maker of the material world, thou Holy one! Which is the fifth place where the Earth feels sorest grief? Ahura Mazda answered: 'It is the place whereon the wife and children of one of the faithful, O Spitama Zarathushtra! are driven along the way of captivity, the dry, the dusty way, and lift up a voice of wailing.'

12.
O Maker of the material world, thou Holy one! Who is the first that rejoices the Earth with greatest joy? Ahura Mazda answered: 'It is he who digs out of it most corpses of dogs and men.' See 8 above.

13.
O Maker of the material world, thou Holy one! Who is the second that rejoices the Earth with greatest joy? Ahura Mazda answered: 'It is he who pulls down most of those Dakhmas on which the corpses of men are deposited.'

14.
Let no man alone by himself carry a corpse. If a man alone by himself carry a corpse, the Nasu rushes upon him, to defile him, from the nose of the dead, from the eye, from the tongue, from the jaws, from the sexual organs, from the hinder parts. This Druj Nasu falls upon him, [stains him] even to the end of the nails, and he is unclean, thenceforth, for ever and ever.

15.
O Maker of the material world, thou Holy one! What shall be the place of that man who has carried a corpse [alone]? Ahura Mazda answered: 'It shall be the place on this earth wherein is least water and fewest plants, whereof the ground is the cleanest

AVESTA: Vendidad

and the dryest and the least passed through by flocks and herds, by the fire of Ahura Mazda, by the consecrated bundles of Baresma, and by the faithful.'

16.

O Maker of the material world, thou Holy one! How far from the fire? How far from the water? How far from the consecrated bundles of Baresma? How far from the faithful?

17.

Ahura Mazda answered: 'Thirty paces from the fire, thirty paces from the water, thirty paces from the consecrated bundles of Baresma, three paces from the faithful.

18,19.

'There, on that place, shall the worshippers of Mazda erect an enclosure, and therein shall they establish him with food, therein shall they establish him with clothes, with the coarsest food and with the most worn-out clothes. That food he shall live on, those clothes he shall wear, and thus shall they let him live, until he has grown to the age of a Hana, or of a Zaurura, or of a Pairishta-khshudra.

20,21.

'And when he has grown to the age of a Hana, or of a Zaurura, or of a Pairishta-khshudra, then the worshippers of Mazda shall order a man strong, vigorous, and skillful 'Trained to operations of that sort' (Comm.), to cut the head off his neck, in his enclosure on the top of the mountain: and they shall deliver his corpse unto the greediest of the corpse-eating creatures made by the beneficent Spirit, unto the vultures, with these words: "The man here has repented of all his evil thoughts, words, and deeds. If he has committed any other evil deed, it is remitted by his repentance: if he has committed no other evil deed, he is absolved by his repentance, for ever and ever."'

22.

O Maker of the material world, thou Holy one! Who is the third that rejoices the Earth with greatest joy? Ahura Mazda answered: 'It is he who fills up most burrows of the creatures of Angra Mainyu.'

AVESTA: Vendidad

23.
O Maker of the material world, thou Holy one! Who is the fourth that rejoices the Earth with greatest joy? Ahura Mazda answered: 'It is he who sows most corn, grass, and fruit, O Spitama Zarathushtra! who waters ground that is dry, or drains ground that is too wet.

24.
'Unhappy is the land that has long lain unsown with the seed of the sower and wants a good husbandman, like a well-shapen maiden who has long gone childless and wants a good husband.

25.
'He who would till the earth, O Spitama Zarathushtra! with the left arm and the right, with the right arm and the left, unto him will she bring forth plenty of fruit: even as it were a lover sleeping with his bride on her bed; the bride will bring forth children, (the earth will bring forth) plenty of fruit.

26,27.
'He who would till the earth, O Spitama Zarathushtra! with the left arm and the right, with the right arm and the left, unto him thus says the Earth: "O thou man! who dost till me with the left arm and the right, with the right arm and the left, here shall I ever go on bearing, bringing forth all manner of food, bringing corn first to thee 'When something good grows up, it will grow up for thee first' (Comm.) Perhaps: 'bringing to thee profusion of corn' ('some say, she will bring to thee 15 for 10;' Comm.) ."

28,29.
'He who does not till the earth, O Spitama Zarathushtra! with the left arm and the right, with the right arm and the left, unto him thus says the Earth: "O thou man! who dost not till me with the left arm and the right, with the right arm and the left, ever shalt thou stand at the door of the stranger, among those who beg for bread; the refuse and the crumbs of the bread are brought unto thee 'They take for themselves what is good and send to thee what is bad' (Comm.) , brought by those who have profusion of wealth."'

30.

AVESTA: Vendidad

O Maker of the material world, thou Holy one! What is the
food that fills the Religion of Mazda [lit: what is the stomach
of the law?]? Ahura Mazda answered: 'It is sowing corn again and
again, O Spitama Zarathushtra!

31.

'He who sows corn, sows righteousness: he makes the Religion
of Mazda walk, he suckles the Religion of Mazda; as well as he
could do with a hundred man's feet, with a thousand woman's breasts 'He
makes the Religion of Mazda as fat as a child could be made by
means of a hundred feet, that is to say, of fifty servants walking
to rock him; of a thousand breasts, that is, of five hundred nurses'
(Comm.) , with ten thousand sacrificial formulas.

32.

'When barley was created, the Daevas started up; when it grew doubtful ,
then fainted the Daevas' hearts; when the knots came doubtful ,
the Daevas groaned; when the ear came, the Daevas flew away. In
that house the Daevas stay, wherein wheat perishes doubtful .
It is as though red hot iron were turned about in their throats,
when there is plenty of corn doubtful .

33.

'Then let people learn by heart this holy saying: "No
one who does not eat, has strength to do heavy works of holiness,
strength to do works of husbandry, strength to beget children.
By eating every material creature lives, by not eating it dies
away."'

34.

O Maker of the material world, thou Holy one! Who is the fifth
that rejoices the Earth with greatest joy?
Ahura Mazda answered: '[It is he who kindly and piously gives The
Asho–dad or alms. The bracketed clause is from the Vendidad Sada.
to one of the faithful who tills the earth,] O Spitama Zarathushtra!

35.

'He who would not kindly and piously give to one of the faithful
who tills the earth, O Spitama Zarathushtra! Spenta Armaiti will
throw him down into darkness, down into the world of woe, the
world of hell, down into the deep abyss Conjectural

AVESTA: Vendidad

translation. .'

36.
O Maker of the material world, thou Holy one! If a man shall bury in the earth either the corpse of a dog or the corpse of a man, and if he shall not disinter it within half a year, what is the penalty that he shall pay?
Ahura Mazda answered: 'Five hundred stripes with the Aspahe–ashtra, five hundred stripes with the Sraosho–charana.'

37.
O Maker of the material world, thou Holy one! If a man shall bury in the earth either the corpse of a dog or the corpse of a man, and if he shall not disinter it within a year, what is the penalty that he shall pay?
Ahura Mazda answered: 'A thousand stripes with the Aspahe–ashtra, a thousand stripes with the Sraosho–charana.'

38.
O Maker of the material world, thou Holy one! If a man shall bury in the earth either the corpse of a dog or the corpse of a man, and if he shall not disinter it within the second year, what is the penalty for it? What is the atonement for it? What is the cleansing from it?

39.
Ahura Mazda answered: 'For that deed there is nothing that can pay, nothing that can atone, nothing that can cleanse from it; it is a trespass for which there is no atonement, for ever and ever.'

40.
When is it so?
'It is so, if the sinner be a professor of the Religion of Mazda, or one who has been taught in it.
'But if he be not a professor of the Religion of Mazda, nor one who has been taught in it, then his sin is taken from him, if he makes confession of the Religion of Mazda and resolves never to commit again such forbidden deeds.

41.
'The Religion of Mazda indeed, O Spitama Zarathushtra! takes

AVESTA: Vendidad

away from him who makes confession of it the bonds of his sin; it takes away (the sin of) breach of trust Doubtful.
From the commentary it appears that draosha must have meant a different sort of robbery: 'He knows that it is forbidden to steal, but he fancies that robbing the rich to give to the poor is a pious deed' (Comm.) ; it takes away (the sin of) murdering one of the faithful; it takes away (the sin of) deeds for which there is no atonement; it takes away the worst sin of usury; it takes away any sin that may be sinned.
42.
'In the same way the Religion of Mazda, O Spitama Zarathushtra! cleanses the faithful from every evil thought, word, and deed, as a swift-rushing mighty wind cleanses the plain 'From chaff' (Comm.) .
'So let all the deeds he doeth be henceforth good, O Zarathushtra! a full atonement for his sin is effected by means of the Religion of Mazda.'

FARGARD 4. Contracts and offenses

I.
1.
He that does not restore a loan to the man who lent it, steals the thing and robs the man "He is a thief when he takes a view not to restore; he is a robber when, being asked to restore, he answers, I will not" (Comm.) .
This he doeth every day, every night, as long as he keep in his house his neighbour's property, as though it were his own.

Ia.
2.
O Maker of the material world, thou Holy One! How many in

AVESTA: Vendidad

number are thy contracts, O Ahura Mazda? Ahura Mazda answered: 'They are six in number, O holy Zarathushtra. The first is the word-contract; the second is the hand-contract; the third is the contract to the amount of a sheep; the fourth is the contract to the amount of an ox; the fifth is the contract to the amount of a man; the sixth is the contract to the amount of a field, a field in good land, a fruitful one, in good bearing.'

3.
The word-contract is fulfilled by words of mouth. It is canceled by the hand-contract; he shall give as damages the amount of the hand-contract.

4.
The hand-contract is canceled by the sheep-contract; he shall give as damages the amount of the sheep-contract. The sheep-contract is canceled by the ox-contract; he shall give as damages the amount of the ox-contract. The ox-contract is canceled by the man-contract; he shall give as damages the amount of the man-contract. The man-contract is canceled by the field-contract; he shall give as damages the amount of the field-contract.

5.
O Maker of the material world, thou Holy One! If a man break the word-contract, how many are involved in his sin? Ahura Mazda answered: 'His sin makes his Nabanazdishtas answerable for three hundred (years).'

6.
O Maker of the material world, thou Holy One! If a man break the hand-contract, how many are involved in his sin? Ahura Mazda answered: 'His sin makes his Nabanazdishtas answerable for six hundred (years).'

7.
O Maker of the material world, thou Holy One! If a man break the sheep-contract, how many are involved in his sin? Ahura Mazda answered: 'His sin makes his Nabanazdishtas answerable for seven hundred (years).'

8.
O Maker of the material world, thou Holy One! If a man break

AVESTA: Vendidad

the ox-contract, how many are involved in his sin? Ahura Mazda answered: 'His sin makes his Nabanazdishtas answerable for eight hundred (years).'

9.
O Maker of the material world, thou Holy One! If a man break the man-contract, how many are involved in his sin? Ahura Mazda answered: 'His sin makes his Nabanazdishtas answerable for nine hundred (years).'

10.
O Maker of the material world, thou Holy One! If a man break the field-contract, how many are involved in his sin? Ahura Mazda answered: 'His sin makes his Nabanazdishtas answerable for a thousand (years).'

11.
O Maker of the material world, thou Holy One! If a man break the word-contract, what is the penalty that he shall pay? Ahura Mazda answered: 'Three hundred stripes with the Aspahe-ashtra, three hundred stripes with the Sraosho-charana.'

12.
O Maker of the material world, thou Holy One! If a man break the hand-contract, what is the penalty that he shall pay? Ahura Mazda answered: 'Six hundred stripes with the Aspahe-ashtra, six hundred stripes with the Sraosho-charana.'

13.
O Maker of the material world, thou Holy One! If a man break the sheep-contract, what is the penalty that he shall pay? Ahura Mazda answered: 'Seven hundred stripes with the Aspahe-ashtra, seven hundred stripes with the Sraosho-charana.'

14.
O Maker of the material world, thou Holy One! If a man break the ox-contract, what is the penalty that he shall pay? Ahura Mazda answered: 'Eight hundred stripes with the Aspahe-ashtra, eight hundred stripes with the Sraosho-charana.'

15.
O Maker of the material world, thou Holy One! If a man break the man-contract, what is the penalty that he shall pay? Ahura

AVESTA: Vendidad

Mazda answered: 'Nine hundred stripes with the Aspahe–ashtra, Nine hundred stripes with the Sraosho–charana.'

16.
O Maker of the material world, thou Holy One! If a man break the field–contract, what is the penalty that he shall pay? Ahura Mazda answered: 'A thousand stripes with the Aspahe–ashtra, a thousand stripes with the Sraosho–charana.'

IIa.
17.
If a man rise up with a weapon in his hand, it is an Agerepta. If he brandish it, it is an Avaoirishta. If he actually smite a man with malicious aforethought, it is an Aredush. Upon the fifth Aredush he becomes a Peshotanu.

18.
O Maker of the material world, thou Holy One! He that committeth an Agerepta, what penalty shall he pay? Ahura Mazda answered: 'Five stripes with the Aspahe–ashtra, five stripes with the Sraosho–charana;

'On the second Agerepta, ten stripes with the Aspahe–ashtra, ten stripes with the Sraosho–charana;
'On the third, fifteen stripes with the Aspahe–ashtra, fifteen stripes with the Sraosho–charana;

19.
'On the fourth, thirty stripes with the Aspahe–ashtra, thirty stripes with the Sraosho–charana;
'On the fifth, fifty stripes with the Aspahe–ashtra, fifty stripes with the Sraosho–charana;
'On the sixth, sixty stripes with the Aspahe–ashtra, sixty stripes with the Sraosho–charana;
'On the seventh, ninety stripes with the Aspahe–ashtra, ninety stripes with the Sraosho–charana.'

20.
If a man commit an Agerepta for the eighth time, without having atoned for the preceding, what penalty shall he pay?

AVESTA: Vendidad

Ahura Mazda answered: 'He is a Peshotanu: two hundred stripes with the Aspahe-ashtra, two hundred stripes with the Sraosho-charana.'
21.
If a man commit an Agerepta, and refuse to atone for it, what penalty shall he pay? Ahura Mazda answered: 'He is a Peshotanu: two hundred stripes with the Aspahe-ashtra, two hundred stripes with the Sraosho-charana.'
22.
O Maker of the material world, thou Holy One! If a man commit an Avaoirishta, what penalty shall he pay? Ahura Mazda answered: 'Ten stripes with the Aspahe-ashtra, ten stripes with the Sraosho-charana;

'On the second Avaoirishta, fifteen stripes with the Aspahe-ashtra, fifteen stripes with the Sraosho-charana;
23.
'On the third, thirty stripes with the Aspahe-ashtra, thirty stripes with the Sraosho-charana;
'On the fourth, fifty stripes with the Aspahe-ashtra, fifty stripes with the Sraosho-charana;
'On the fifth, seventy stripes with the Aspahe-ashtra, seventy stripes with the Sraosho-charana;
'On the sixth, ninety stripes with the Aspahe-ashtra, ninety stripes with the Sraosho-charana.'
24.
O Maker of the material world, thou Holy One! If a man commit an Avaoirishta for the seventh time, without having atoned for the preceding, what penalty shall he pay? Ahura Mazda answered: 'He is a Peshotanu: two hundred stripes with the Aspahe-ashtra, two hundred stripes with the Sraosho-charana.'
25.
O Maker of the material world, thou Holy One! If a man commit an Avaoirishta, and refuse to atone for it, what penalty shall he pay? Ahura Mazda answered: 'He is a Peshotanu: two hundred stripes with the Aspahe-ashtra, two hundred stripes with the Sraosho-charana.'
26.
O Maker of the material world, thou Holy One! If a man commit

AVESTA: Vendidad

an Aredush, what penalty shall he pay? Ahura Mazda answered: 'Fifteen stripes with the Aspahe-ashtra, fifteen stripes with the Sraosho-charana;

27.
'On the second Aredush, thirty stripes with the Aspahe-ashtra, thirty stripes with the Sraosho-charana;
'On the third, fifty stripes with the Aspahe-ashtra, fifty stripes with the Sraosho-charana;
'On the fourth, seventy stripes with the Aspahe-ashtra, seventy stripes with the Sraosho-charana;
'On the fifth, ninety stripes with the Aspahe-ashtra, ninety stripes with the Sraosho-charana;

28.
O Maker of the material world, thou Holy One! If a man commit an Aredush for the sixth time, without having atoned for the preceding, what penalty shall he pay? Ahura Mazda answered: 'He is a Peshotanu: two hundred stripes with the Aspahe-ashtra, two hundred stripes with the Sraosho-charana.'

29.
O Maker of the material world, thou Holy One! If a man commit an Aredush, and refuse to atone for it, what penalty shall he pay? Ahura Mazda answered: 'He is a Peshotanu: two hundred stripes with the Aspahe-ashtra, two hundred stripes with the Sraosho-charana.'

30.
O Maker of the material world, thou Holy One! If a man smite another and hurt him sorely, what is the penalty that he shall pay?

31.
Ahura Mazda answered: 'Thirty stripes with the Aspahe-ashtra, thirty stripes with the Sraosho-charana;
'The second time, fifty stripes with the Aspahe-ashtra, fifty stripes with the Sraosho-charana;
'The third time, seventy stripes with the Aspahe-ashtra, seventy stripes with the Sraosho-charana;
'The fourth time, ninety stripes with the Aspahe-ashtra, ninety stripes with the Sraosho-charana;

32.

AVESTA: Vendidad

If a man commit that deed for the fifth time, without having atoned for the preceding, what penalty shall he pay? Ahura Mazda answered: 'He is a Peshotanu: two hundred stripes with the Aspahe–ashtra, two hundred stripes with the Sraosho–charana.'

33.

If a man commit that deed and refuse to atone for it, what penalty shall he pay? Ahura Mazda answered: 'He is a Peshotanu: two hundred stripes with the Aspahe–ashtra, two hundred stripes with the Sraosho–charana.'

34.

O Maker of the material world, thou Holy One! If a man smite another so that the blood come, what is the penalty that he shall pay? Ahura Mazda answered: 'Fifty stripes with the Aspahe–ashtra, fifty stripes with the Sraosho–charana;

'The second time, seventy stripes with the Aspahe–ashtra, seventy stripes with the Sraosho–charana;

'The third time, ninety stripes with the Aspahe–ashtra, ninety stripes with the Sraosho–charana;

35.

If a man commit that deed for the fourth time, without having atoned for the preceding, what penalty shall he pay? Ahura Mazda answered: 'He is a Peshotanu: two hundred stripes with the Aspahe–ashtra, two hundred stripes with the Sraosho–charana.'

36.

O Maker of the material world, thou Holy One! If a man smite another so that the blood come, and if he refuse to atone for it, what penalty shall he pay? Ahura Mazda answered: 'He is a Peshotanu: two hundred stripes with the Aspahe–ashtra, two hundred stripes with the Sraosho–charana.'

37.

O Maker of the material world, thou Holy One! If a man smite another so that he break a bone, what is the penalty that he shall pay? Ahura Mazda answered: 'Seventy stripes with the Aspahe–ashtra, seventy stripes with the Sraosho–charana;

'The second time, ninety stripes with the Aspahe–ashtra, ninety stripes with the Sraosho–charana;

AVESTA: Vendidad

38.
If he commit that deed for the third time, without having atoned for the preceding, what penalty shall he pay? Ahura Mazda answered: 'He is a Peshotanu: two hundred stripes with the Aspahe-ashtra, two hundred stripes with the Sraosho-charana.'

39.
O Maker of the material world, thou Holy One! If a man smite another so that he break a bone, and if he refuse to atone for it, what is the penalty he shall pay? Ahura Mazda answered: 'He is a Peshotanu: two hundred stripes with the Aspahe-ashtra, two hundred stripes with the Sraosho-charana.'

40.
O Maker of the material world, thou Holy One! If a man smite another so that he give up the ghost, what is the penalty that he shall pay? Ahura Mazda answered: 'Ninety stripes with the Aspahe-ashtra, seventy stripes with the Sraosho-charana;

41.
If he commit that deed again, without having atoned for the preceding, what is the penalty that he shall pay? Ahura Mazda answered: 'He is a Peshotanu: two hundred stripes with the Aspahe-ashtra, two hundred stripes with the Sraosho-charana.'

42.
O Maker of the material world, thou Holy One! If a man smite another so that he give up the ghost, and if he refuse to atone for it, what is the penalty he shall pay? Ahura Mazda answered: 'He is a Peshotanu: two hundred stripes with the Aspahe-ashtra, two hundred stripes with the Sraosho-charana.'

43.
And they shall thenceforth in their doings walk after the way of holiness, after the word of holiness, after the ordinance of holiness.

IIIa.
44.
If men of the same faith, either friends or brothers, come

AVESTA: Vendidad

to an agreement together, that one may obtain from the other,
either goods, or a wife, or knowledge, let him who desires goods
have them delivered to him; let him who desires a wife receive
and wed her; let him who desires knowledge be taught the holy
word,

45.

during the first part of the day and the last, during the
first part of the night and the last, that his mind may be increased
in intelligence and wax strong in holiness. So shall he sit up,
in devotion and prayers, that he may be increased in intelligence:
he shall rest during the middle part of the day, during the middle
part of the night, and thus shall he continue until he can say
all the words which former Aethrapaitis have said.

IVa.
46.
Before the boiling water publicly prepared This
clause is intended against false oaths taken in the so-called
Var-ordeal (see par. 54 n.) It ought to be placed before par.
49 bis, where the penalty for a false oath is given. ,
O Spitama Zarathushtra! let no one make bold to deny having received
[from his neighbor] the ox or the garment in his possession.
47.
Verily I say it unto thee, O Spitama Zarathushtra! the man
who has a wife is far above him who lives in continence; he who
keeps a house is far above him who has none; he who has children
is far above the childless man; he who has riches is far above
him who has none.
48.
And of two men, he who fills himself with meat receives in
him Vohu Mano much better than he who does not do so; the latter
is all but dead; the former is above him by the worth of an Asperena,
by the worth of a sheep, by the worth of an ox, by the worth of
a man.
49.

AVESTA: Vendidad

This man can strive against the onsets of Asto-vidhotu; he can strive against the well-darted arrow; he can strive against the winter fiend, with thinnest garment on; he can strive against the wicked tyrant and smite him on the head; he can strive against the ungodly fasting Ashemaogha.

IVb.
49 (bis).
On the very first time when that deed has been done, without waiting until it is done again,
50.
down there In hell. the pain for
that deed shall be as hard as any in this world: even as if one should cut off the limbs from his perishable body with knives of brass, or still worse;
51.
down there the pain for that deed shall be as hard as any in this world: even as if one should nail doubtful his perishable body with nails of brass, or still worse;
52.
down there the pain for that deed shall be as hard as any in this world: even as if one should by force throw his perishable body headlong down a precipice a hundred times the height of a man, or still worse;
53.
down there the pain for that deed shall be as hard as any in this world: even as if one should by force impale doubtful his perishable body, or still worse.
54.
Down there the pain for that deed shall be as hard as any in this world: to wit, the deed of a man, who knowingly lying, confronts the brimstoned, golden, truth-knowing water with an appeal unto Rashnu and a lie unto Mithra.
55.
O Maker of the material world, thou Holy One! He who, knowingly

AVESTA: Vendidad

lying, confronts the brimstoned, golden, truth-knowing water with an appeal unto Rashnu and a lie unto Mithra, what is the penalty that he shall pay In this world. ? Ahura
Mazda answered: 'Seven hundred stripes with the Aspahe-ashtra, seven hundred stripes with the Sraosho-charana.'

FARGARD 5. Purity laws

I
1.
There dies a man in the depths of the vale: a bird takes flight from the top of the mountain down into the depths of the vale, and it feeds on the corpse of the dead man there: then, up it flies from the depths of the vale to the top of the mountain: it flies to some one of the trees there, of the hard-wooded or the soft-wooded, and upon that tree it vomits and deposits dung.
2.
Now, lo! here is a man coming up from the depths of the vale to the top of the mountain; he comes to the tree whereon the bird is sitting; from that tree he intends to take wood for the fire. He fells the tree, he hews the tree, he splits it into logs, and then he lights it in the fire, the son of Ahura Mazda. What is the penalty he shall pay?
3.
Ahura Mazda answered: 'There is no sin upon a man for any Nasu that has been brought by dogs, by birds, by wolves, by winds, or by flies.
4.
'For were there sin upon a man for any Nasu that might have been brought by dogs, by birds, by wolves, by winds, or by flies, how soon all this material world of mine would be only one Peshotanu, bent on the destruction of righteousness, and whose soul will

AVESTA: Vendidad

cry and wail! so numberless are the beings that die upon the face of the earth.'

5.

O Maker of the material world, thou Holy One! Here is a man watering a corn-field. The water streams down the field; it streams again; it streams a third time; and the fourth time, a dog, a fox, or a wolf carries some Nasu into the bed of the stream: what is the penalty that the man shall pay?

6.

[Repeat st. 3.]

7.

[Repeat st. 4.]

8.

O Maker of the material world, thou Holy One! Does water kill? Ahura Mazda answered: 'Water kills no man: Asto-vidhotu binds him, and, thus bound, Vayu carries him off; and the flood takes him up, the flood takes him down, the flood throws him ashore; then birds feed upon him. When he goes away, it is by the will of Fate he goes.'

IIb.

9.

O Maker of the material world, thou Holy One! Does fire kill? Ahura Mazda answered: 'Fire kills no man: Asto-vidhotu binds him, and, thus bound, Vayu carries him off; and the fire burns up life and limb. When he goes away, it is by the will of Fate he goes.'

III.

10.

O Maker of the material world, thou Holy One! If the summer is past and the winter has come, what shall the worshippers of Mazda do? Ahura Mazda answered: 'In every house, in every borough, they shall raise three rooms for the dead.'

11.

AVESTA: Vendidad

O Maker of the material world, thou Holy One! How large shall be those rooms for the dead? Ahura Mazda answered: 'Large enough not to strike the skull of the man, if he should stand erect, or his feet or his hands stretched out: such shall be, according to the law, the rooms for the dead.
12.
'And they shall let the lifeless body lie there, for two nights, or for three nights, or a month long, until the birds begin to fly, the plants to grow, the hidden floods to flow, and the wind to dry up the earth.
13.
'And as soon as the birds begin to fly, the plants to grow, the hidden floods to flow, and the wind to dry up the earth, then the worshippers of Mazda shall lay down the dead (on the Dakhma), his eyes towards the sun.
14.
'If the worshippers of Mazda have not, within a year, laid down the dead (on the Dakhma), his eyes towards the sun, thou shalt prescribe for that trespass the same penalty as for the murder of one of the faithful; until the corpse has been rained on, until the Dakhma has been rained on, until the unclean remains have been rained on, until the birds have eaten up the corpse.'

IV.
15.
O Maker of the material world, thou Holy One! Is it true at thou, Ahura Mazda, seizest the waters from the sea Vouru-kasha with the wind and the clouds?
16.
That thou, Ahura Mazda, takest them down to the corpses? that thou, Ahura Mazda, takest them down to the Dakhmas? that thou, Ahura Mazda, takest them down to the unclean remains? that thou, Ahura Mazda, takest them down to the bones? and that then thou, Ahura Mazda, makest them flow back unseen? that thou, Ahura Mazda, makest them flow back to the sea Puitika?

AVESTA: Vendidad

17.
Ahura Mazda answered: 'It is even so as thou hast said, O righteous Zarathushtra! I, Ahura Mazda, seize the waters from the sea Vouru-kasha with the wind and the clouds.

18.
'I, Ahura Mazda, take them to the corpses; I, Ahura Mazda, take them down to the Dakhmas; I, Ahura Mazda, take them down to the unclean remains; I, Ahura Mazda, take them down to the bones; then I, Ahura Mazda, make them flow back unseen; I, Ahura Mazda, make them flow back to the sea Puitika.

19.
'The waters stand there boiling, boiling up in the heart of the sea Puitika, and, when cleansed there, they run back again from the sea Puitika to the sea Vouru-kasha, towards the well-watered tree, whereon grow the seeds of my plants of every kind by hundreds, by thousands, by hundreds of thousands.

20.
'Those plants, I, Ahura Mazda, rain down upon the earth, to bring food to the faithful, and fodder to the beneficent cow; to bring food to my people that they may live on it, and fodder to the beneficent cow.'

V.

21.
'This is the best, this is the fairest of all things, even as thou hast said, O pure [Zarathushtra]!'
With these words the holy, Ahura Mazda rejoiced the holy Zarathushtra:
'Purity is for man, next to life, the greatest good, that purity, O Zarathushtra, that is in the Religion of Mazda for him who cleanses his own self with good thoughts, words, and deeds.'

22.
O Maker of the material world, thou Holy One! This Law, this fiend-destroying Law of Zarathushtra, by what greatness, goodness, and fairness is it great, good, and fair above all other utterances?

23.

AVESTA: Vendidad

Ahura Mazda answered: 'As much above all other floods as is
the sea Vouru-kasha, so much above all other utterances in greatness,
goodness, and fairness is this Law, this fiend-destroying Law
of Zarathushtra.
24.
'As much as a great stream flows swifter than a slender rivulet,
so much above all other utterances in greatness, goodness, and
fairness is this Law, this fiend-destroying Law of Zarathushtra.

'As high as the great tree stands above the small plants it overshadows,
so high above all other utterances in greatness, goodness, and
fairness is this Law, this fiend-destroying Law of Zarathushtra.
25.
'As high as heaven is above the earth that it compasses around,
so high above all other utterances is this Law, this fiend-destroying
Law of Mazda.
'[Therefore], he will apply to the Ratu, he will apply to the
Sraosha-varez; whether for a draona-service that should have been
undertaken and has not been undertaken; or for a draona that should
have been offered up and has not been offered up; or for a draona
that should have been entrusted and has not been entrusted.
26.
'The Ratu has power to remit him one-third of his penalty:
if he has committed any other evil deed, it is remitted by his
repentance; if he has committed no other evil deed, he is absolved
by his repentance for ever and ever.'

VI.
27.
O Maker of the material world, thou Holy One! If there be
a number of men resting in the same place, on the same carpet,
on the same pillows, be there two men near one another, or five,
or fifty, or a hundred, close by one another; and of those people
one happens to die; how many of them does the Druj Nasu envelope
with corruption, infection, and pollution?

AVESTA: Vendidad

28.
Ahura Mazda answered: 'If the dead one be a priest, the Druj Nasu rushes forth, O Spitama Zarathushtra! she goes as far as the eleventh and defiles the ten.
'If the dead one be a warrior, the Druj Nasu rushes forth, O Spitama Zarathushtra! she goes as far as the tenth and defiles the nine.

'If the dead one be a husbandman, the Druj Nasu rushes forth, O Spitama Zarathushtra! she goes as far as the ninth and defiles the eight.
29.
'If it be a shepherd's dog, the Druj Nasu rushes forth, O Spitama Zarathushtra! she goes as far as the eighth and defiles the seven.
'If it be a house-dog, the Druj Nasu rushes forth, O Spitama Zarathushtra! she goes as far as the seventh and defiles the six.
30.
'If it be a Vohunazga dog, the Druj Nasu rushes forth, O Spitama Zarathushtra! she goes as far as the sixth and defiles the five.

'If it be a Tauruna dog, the Druj Nasu rushes forth, O Spitama Zarathushtra! she goes as far as the fifth and defiles the four.
31.
'If it be a porcupine dog, the Druj Nasu rushes forth, O Spitama Zarathushtra! she goes as far as the fourth and defiles the three.

'If it be a Gazu dog, the Druj Nasu rushes forth, O Spitama Zarathushtra! she goes as far as the third and defiles the two.
32.
'If it be an Aiwizu dog, the Druj Nasu rushes forth, O Spitama Zarathushtra! she goes as far as the second and defiles the next.

'If it be a Vizu dog, the Druj Nasu rushes forth, O Spitama Zarathushtra! she goes as far as the next, she defiles the next.'
33.
O Maker of the material world, thou Holy One! If it be a weasel,

AVESTA: Vendidad

how many of the creatures of the good spirit does it directly defile, how many does it indirectly defile?

34.

Ahura Mazda answered : 'A weasel does neither directly nor indirectly defile any of the creatures of the good spirit, but him who smites and kills it; to him the uncleanness clings for ever and ever.'

35.

O Maker of the material world, thou Holy One! If the dead one be such a wicked, two-footed ruffian, as an ungodly Ashemaogha, how many of the creatures of the good spirit does he directly defile, how many does he indirectly defile?

36.

Ahura Mazda answered: 'No more than a frog does whose venom is dried up, and that has been dead more than a year. Whilst alive, indeed, O Spitama Zarathushtra! such a wicked, two-legged ruffian as an ungodly Ashemaogha, directly defiles the creatures of the good spirit, and indirectly defiles them.

37.

'Whilst alive he smites the water; whilst alive he blows out the fire; whilst alive he carries off the cow; whilst alive he smites the faithful man with a deadly blow, that parts the soul from the body; not so will he do when dead.

38.

'Whilst alive, indeed, O Spitama Zarathushtra! such a wicked, two-legged ruffian as an ungodly Ashemaogha robs the faithful man of the full possession of his food, of his clothing, of his wood, of his bed, of his vessels; not so will he do when dead.'

VII.

39.

O Maker of the material world, thou Holy One! When into our houses here below we have brought the fire, the Baresma, the cups, the Haoma, and the mortar, O holy Ahura Mazda! if it come to pass that either a dog or a man dies there, what shall the worshippers

AVESTA: Vendidad

of Mazda do?

40.

Ahura Mazda answered: 'Out of the house, O Spitama Zarathushtra! shall they take the fire, the Baresma, the cups, the Haoma, and the mortar; they shall take the dead one out to the proper place whereto, according to the law, corpses must be brought, to be devoured there.'

41.

O Maker of the material world, thou Holy One! When shall they bring back the fire into the house wherein the man has died? 42. Ahura Mazda answered: 'They shall wait for nine nights in winter, for a month in summer, and then they shall bring back the fire to the house wherein the man has died.'

43.

O Maker of the material world, thou Holy One! And if they shall bring back the fire to the house wherein the man has died, within the nine nights, or within the month, what penalty shall they pay?

44.

Ahura Mazda answered: 'They shall be Peshotanus: two hundred stripes with the Aspahe-astra, two hundred stripes with the Sraosho-karana.'

VIII.

45.

O Maker of the material world, thou Holy One! If in the house of a worshipper of Mazda there be a woman with child, and if being a month gone, or two, or three, or four, or five, or six, or seven, or eight, or nine, or ten months gone, she bring forth a still-born child, what shall the worshippers of Mazda do?

46.

Ahura Mazda answered: 'The place in that Mazdean house whereof the ground is the cleanest and the driest, and the least passed through by flocks and herds, by the fire of Ahura Mazda, by the consecrated bundles of Baresma, and by the faithful;'

47.

AVESTA: Vendidad

O Maker of the material world, thou Holy One! How far from the fire? How far from the water? How far from the consecrated bundles of Baresma? How far from the faithful?
48.
Ahura Mazda answered: 'Thirty paces from the fire; thirty paces from the water; thirty paces from the consecrated bundles of Baresma; three paces from the faithful;–
49.
'On that place shall the worshippers of Mazda erect an enclosure, and therein shall they establish her with food, therein shall they establish her with clothes.'
50.
O Maker of the material world, thou Holy One! What is the food that the woman shall first take?
51.
Ahura Mazda answered: 'Gomez mixed with ashes, three draughts of it, or six, or nine, to send down the Dakhma within her womb.
52.
'Afterwards she may drink boiling milk of mares, cows, sheep, or goats, with pap or without pap; she may take cooked milk without water, meal without water, and wine without water.'
53.
O Maker of the material world, thou Holy One! How long shall she remain so? How long shall she live thus on milk, meal, and wine?
54.
Ahura Mazda answered: 'Three nights long shall she remain so; three nights long shall she live thus on milk, meal, and wine. Then, when three nights have passed, she shall wash her body, she shall wash her clothes, with gomez and water, by the nine holes, and thus shall she be clean.'
55.
O Maker of the material world, thou Holy One! How long shall she remain so? How long, after the three nights have gone, shall she sit confined, and live separated from the rest of the worshippers of Mazda, as to her seat, her food, and her clothing?

AVESTA: Vendidad

56.
Ahura Mazda answered: 'Nine nights long shall she remain so: nine nights long, after the three nights have gone, shall she sit confined, and live separated from the rest of the worshippers of Mazda, as to her seat, her food, and her clothing. Then, when the nine nights have gone, she shall wash her body, and cleanse her clothes with gomez and water.'

57.
O Maker of the material world, thou Holy One! Can those clothes, when once washed and cleansed, ever be used either by a Zaotar, or by a Havanan, or by an Atare-vakhsha, or by a Frabaretar, or by an Abered, or by an Asnatar, or by a Rathwishkar, or by a Sraosha-varez, or by any priest, warrior, or husbandman?

58.
Ahura Mazda answered: 'Never can those clothes, even when washed and cleansed, be used either by a Zaotar, or by a Havanan, or by an Atare-vakhsha, or by a Frabaretar, or by an Abered, or by an Asnatar, or by a Rathwishkar, or by a Sraosha-varez, or by any priest, warrior, or husbandman.

59.
'But if there be in a Mazdean house a woman who is in her sickness, or a man who has become unfit for work, and who must sit in the place of infirmity, those clothes shall serve for their coverings and for their sheets, until they can withdraw their hands for prayer.

60.
'Ahura Mazda, indeed, does not allow us to waste anything of value that we may have, not even so much as an Asperena's weight of thread, not even so much as a maid lets fall in spinning.

61.
'Whosoever throws any clothing on a dead body, even so much as a maid lets fall in spinning, is not a pious man whilst alive, nor shall he, when dead, have a place in Paradise.

62.
'He makes himself a viaticum unto the world of the wicked, into that world, made of darkness, the offspring of darkness,

which is Darkness' self. To that world, to the world of Hell, you are delivered by your own doings, by your own religion, O sinners!'

FARGARD 6. Purity laws

I.
1.
How long shall the piece of ground he fallow whereon dogs or men have died? Ahura Mazda answered: 'A year long shall the piece of ground he fallow whereon dogs or men have died, O holy Zarathushtra!
2.
'A year long shall no worshipper of Mazda sow or water that piece of ground whereon dogs or men have died; he may sow as he likes the rest of the ground; he may water it as he likes.
3.
'If within the year they shall sow or water the piece of ground whereon dogs or men have died, they are guilty of the sin of "burying the dead" towards the water, towards the earth, and towards the plants.'
4.
O Maker of the material world, thou Holy One! If worshippers of Mazda shall sow or water, within the year, the piece of ground whereon dogs or men have died, what is the penalty that they shall pay?
5.
Ahura Mazda answered: 'They are Peshotanus: two hundred stripes with the Aspahe–astra, two hundred stripes with the Sraosho–karana.'
6.
O Maker of the material world, thou Holy One! If worshippers of Mazda want to till that piece of ground again, to water it,

AVESTA: Vendidad

to sow it, and to plough it, what shall they do?

7.
Ahura Mazda answered: 'They shall look on the ground for any bones, hair, dung, urine, or blood that may be there.'

8.
O Maker of the material world, thou Holy One! If they shall not look on the ground for any bones, hair, dung, urine, or blood that may be there, what is the penalty that they shall pay?

9.
Ahura Mazda answered: 'They are Peshotanus: two hundred stripes with the Aspahe-astra, two hundred stripes with the Sraosho-karana.'

II.
10.
O Maker of the material world, thou Holy One! If a man shall throw on the ground a bone of a dead dog, or of a dead man, as large as the top joint of the little finger, and if grease or marrow flow from it on to the ground, what penalty shall he pay?

11.
Ahura Mazda answered: 'Thirty stripes with the Aspahe-astra, thirty stripes with the Sraosho-karana.'

12.
O Maker of the material world, thou Holy One! If a man shall throw on the ground a bone of a dead dog, or of a dead man, as large as the top joint of the fore-finger, and if grease or marrow flow from it on to the ground, what penalty shall he pay?

13.
Ahura Mazda answered: 'Fifty stripes with the Aspahe-astra, fifty stripes with the Sraosho-karana.'

14.
O Maker of the material world, thou Holy One! If a man shall throw on the ground a bone of a dead dog, or of a dead man, as large as the top joint of the middle finger, and if grease or marrow flow from it on to the ground, what penalty shall he pay?

15.

AVESTA: Vendidad

Ahura Mazda answered: 'Seventy stripes with the Aspahe-astra, seventy stripes with the Sraosho-karana.'

16.

O Maker of the material world, thou Holy One! If a man shall throw on the ground a bone of a dead dog, or of a dead man, as large as a finger or as a rib, and if grease or marrow flow from it on to the ground, what penalty shall he pay?

17.

Ahura Mazda answered: 'Ninety stripes with the Aspahe-astra, ninety stripes with the Sraosho-charana.'

18.

O Maker of the material world, thou Holy One! If a man shall throw on the ground a bone of a dead dog, or of a dead man, as large as two fingers or as two ribs, and if grease or marrow flow from it on the ground, what penalty shall he pay?

19.

Ahura Mazda answered: 'He is Peshotanu: two hundred stripes with the Aspahe-ashtra, two hundred stripes with the Sraosho-charana.'

20.

O Maker of the material world, thou Holy One! If a man shall throw on the ground a bone of a dead dog, or of a dead man, as large as an arm-bone or as a thigh-bone, and if grease or marrow flow from it on the ground, what penalty shall he pay?

21.

Ahura Mazda answered: 'Four hundred stripes with the Aspahe-ashtra, four hundred stripes with the Sraosho-charana.'

22.

O Maker of the material world, thou Holy One! If a man shall throw on the ground a bone of a dead dog, or of a dead man, as large as a man's skull, and if grease or marrow flow from it on the ground, what penalty shall he pay?

23.

Ahura Mazda answered: 'Six hundred stripes with the Aspahe-ashtra, six hundred stripes with the Sraosho-charana.'

24.

O Maker of the material world, thou Holy One! If a man shall

AVESTA: Vendidad

throw on the ground the whole body of a dead dog, or of a dead man, and if grease or marrow flow from it on the ground, what penalty shall he pay?

25.
Ahura Mazda answered: 'A thousand stripes with the Aspahe-ashtra, a thousand stripes with the Sraosho-charana.'

III.
26.
O Maker of the material world, thou Holy One! If a worshipper of Mazda, walking, or running, or riding, or driving, come upon a corpse in a stream of running water, what shall he do?

27.
Ahura Mazda answered: 'Taking off his shoes, putting off his clothes, while the others wait, O Zarathushtra! he shall enter the river, and take the dead out of the water; he shall go down into the water ankle-deep, knee-deep, waist-deep, or a man's full depth, till he can reach the dead body.'

28.
O Maker of the material world, thou Holy One! If, however, the body be already falling to pieces and rotting, what shall the worshipper of Mazda do?

29.
Ahura Mazda answered: 'He shall draw out of the water as much of the corpse as he can grasp with both hands, and he shall lay it down on the dry ground; no sin attaches to him for any bone, hair, grease, dung, urine, or blood that may drop back into the water.'

30.
O Maker of the material world, thou Holy One! What part of the water in a pond does the Druj Nasu defile with corruption, infection, and pollution?

31.
Ahura Mazda answered: 'Six steps on each of the four sides. As long as the corpse has not been taken out of the water, so

AVESTA: Vendidad

long shall that water be unclean and unfit to drink. They shall, therefore, take the corpse out of the pond, and lay it down on the dry ground.

32.

'And of the water they shall draw off the half, or the third, or the fourth, or the fifth part, according as they are able or not; and after the corpse has been taken out and the water has been drawn off, the rest of the water is clean, and both cattle and men may drink of it at their pleasure, as before.'

33.

O Maker of the material world, thou Holy One! What part of the water in a well does the Druj Nasu defile with corruption, infection, and pollution?

34.

Ahura Mazda answered: 'As long as the corpse has not been taken out of the water, so long shall that water be unclean and unfit to drink. They shall, therefore, take the corpse out of the well, and lay it down on the dry ground.

35.

'And of the water in the well they shall draw off the half, or the third, or the fourth, or the fifth part, according as they are able or not; and after the corpse has been taken out and the water has been drawn off, the rest of the water is clean, and both cattle and men may drink of it at their pleasure, as before.'

36.

O Maker of the material world, thou Holy One! What part of a sheet of snow or hail does the Druj Nasu defile with corruption, infection, and pollution?

37.

Ahura Mazda answered: 'Three steps on each of the four sides. As long as the corpse has not been taken out of the water, so long shall that water be unclean and unfit to drink. They shall, therefore, take the corpse out of the pond, and lay it down on the dry ground.

38.

'After the corpse has been taken out, and the snow or the

AVESTA: Vendidad

hail has melted, the water is clean, and both cattle and men may drink of it at their pleasure, as before.'

39.
O Maker of the material world, thou Holy One! What part of the water of a running stream does the Druj Nasu defile with corruption, infection, and pollution?

40.
Ahura Mazda answered: 'Three steps down the stream, nine steps up the stream, six steps across. As long as the corpse has not been taken out of the water, so long shall that water be unclean and unfit to drink. They shall, therefore, take the corpse out of the pond, and lay it down on the dry ground.

41.
'After the corpse has been taken out and the stream has flowed three times, the water is clean, and both cattle and men may drink of it at their pleasure, as before.'

IV.
42.
O Maker of the material world, thou Holy One! Can the Haoma that has been touched with Nasu from a dead dog, or from a dead man, be made clean again?

43.
Ahura Mazda answered: 'It can, O holy Zarathushtra! If it has been prepared for the sacrifice, there is to it no corruption, no death, no touch of any Nasu. If it has not been prepared for the sacrifice, [the stem] is defiled the length of four fingers: it shall be laid down on the ground, in the middle of the house, for a year long. When the year is passed, the faithful may drink of its juice at their pleasure, as before.'

V.
44.
O Maker of the material world, thou holy One! Whither shall

AVESTA: Vendidad

we bring, where shall we lay the bodies of the dead, O Ahura Mazda?
45.
Ahura Mazda answered: 'On the highest summits, where they know there are always corpse–eating dogs and corpse–eating birds, O holy Zarathushtra!
46.
'There shall the worshippers of Mazda fasten the corpse, by the feet and by the hair, with brass, stones, or clay, lest the corpse–eating dogs and the corpse–eating birds shall go and carry the bones to the water and to the trees.
47.
'If they shall not fasten the corpse, so that the corpse–eating dogs and the corpse–eating birds may go and carry the bones to the water and to the trees, what is the penalty that they shall pay?'
48.
Ahura Mazda answered: 'They shall be Peshotanus: two hundred stripes with the Aspahe–ashtra, two hundred stripes with the Sraosho–charana.'
49.
O Maker of the material world, thou Holy One! Whither shall we bring, where shall we lay the bones of the dead, O Ahura Mazda?
50.
Ahura Mazda answered: 'The worshippers of Mazda shall make a receptacle out of the reach of the dog, of the fox, and of the wolf, and wherein rain–water cannot stay.
51.
'They shall make it, if they can afford it, with stones, plaster, or earth; if they cannot afford it, they shall lay down the dead man on the ground, on his carpet and his pillow, clothed with the light of heaven, and beholding the sun.'

AVESTA: Vendidad

FARGARD 7. Purity laws

I.
1.
Zarathushtra asked Ahura Mazda: 'O Ahura Mazda, most beneficent Spirit, Maker of the material world, thou Holy One! When a man dies, at what moment does the Druj Nasu rush upon him?'
2.
Ahura Mazda answered: 'Directly after death, as soon as the soul has left the body, O Spitama Zarathushtra! the Druj Nasu comes and rushes upon him, from the regions of the north, in the shape of a raging fly, with knees and tail sticking out, droning without end, and like unto the foulest Khrafstras.
[3.
'On him she stays until the dog has seen the corpse or eaten it up, or until the flesh-eating birds have taken flight towards it. When the dog has seen it or eaten it up, or when the flesh-eating birds have taken flight towards it, then the Druj Nasu rushes away to the regions of the north in the shape of a raging fly, with knees and tail sticking out, droning without end, and like unto the foulest Khrafstras.']
4.
O Maker of the material world, thou Holy One! If the man has been killed by a dog, or by a wolf, or by witchcraft, or by the artifices of hatred, or by falling down a precipice, or by the law, or by calumny, or by the noose, how long after death does the Druj Nasu come and rush upon the dead?
5.
Ahura Mazda answered: 'At the next watch after death, the Druj Nasu comes and rushes upon the dead, from the regions of the north, in the shape of a raging fly, with knees and tail sticking out, droning without end, and like unto the foulest Khrafstras.'

AVESTA: Vendidad

II.

6.
O Maker of the material world, thou Holy One! If there be a number of men resting in the same place, on the same carpet, on the same pillows, be there two men near one another, or five, or fifty, or a hundred, close by one another; and of those people one happens to die; how many of them does the Druj Nasu envelope with corruption, infection, and pollution? 7. Ahura Mazda answered: 'If the dead one be a priest, the Druj Nasu rushes forth, O Spitama Zarathushtra! she goes as far as the eleventh and defiles the ten.

'If the dead one he a warrior, the Druj Nasu rushes forth, O Spitama Zarathushtra! she goes as far as the tenth and defiles the nine.

'If the dead one be a husbandman, the Druj Nasu rushes forth, O Spitama Zarathushtra! she goes as far as the ninth and defiles the eight.

8.
'If it be a shepherd's dog, the Druj Nasu rushes forth, O Spitama Zarathushtra! she goes as far as the eighth and defiles the seven.

'If it be a house dog, the Druj Nasu rushes forth, O Spitama Zarathushtra! she goes as far as the seventh and defiles the six. 9. 'If it he a Vohunazga dog, the Druj Nasu rushes forth, O Spitama Zarathushtra! she goes as far as the sixth and defiles the five.

'If it be a Tauruna dog, the Druj Nasu rushes forth, O Spitama Zarathushtra! she goes as far as the fifth and defiles the four.'
. . . 'Those clothes shall serve for their coverings and for their sheets.'. . .

III.

10.
O Maker of the material world, thou Holy One! What part of his bedding and pillow does the Druj Nasu defile with corruption, infection, and pollution?

AVESTA: Vendidad

11.
Ahura Mazda answered: 'The Druj Nasu defiles with corruption, infection, and pollution the upper sheet and the inner garment.'

12.
O Maker of the material world, thou Holy One! Can that garment be made clean, O holy Ahura Mazda! that has been touched by the carcass of a dog or the corpse of a man?

13.
Ahura Mazda answered: 'It can, O holy Zarathushtra!'
How so?
'If there be on the garment seed, or blood, or dirt, or vomit, the worshippers of Mazda shall rend it to pieces, and bury it under the ground.

14.
'But if there be no seed [on the garment], nor blood, nor dirt, nor vomit, then the worshippers of Mazda shall wash it with gomez.

15.
'If it be leather, they shall wash it with gomez three times, they shall rub it with earth three times, they shall wash it with water three times, and afterwards they shall expose it to the air for three months at the window of the house.
'If it be woven cloth, they shall wash it with gomez six times, they shall rub it with earth six times, they shall wash it with water six times, and afterwards they shall expose it to the air for six months at the window of the house.

16.
'The spring named Ardvi Sura, O Spitama Zarathushtra! that spring of mine, purifies the seed of males, the womb of females, the milk of females.'

17.
O Maker of the material world, thou Holy One! Can those clothes, when once washed and cleansed, ever be used either by a Zaotar, or by a Havanan, or by an Atare–vakhsha, or by a Frabaretar, or by an Abered, or by an Asnatar, or by a Rathwishkar, or by a Sraosha–varez, or by any priest, warrior, or husbandman?

AVESTA: Vendidad

18.
Ahura Mazda answered: 'Never can those clothes, even when washed and cleansed, be used either by a Zaotar, or by a Havanan, or by an Atare-vakhsha, or by a Frabaretar, or by an Abered, or by an Asnatar, or by a Rathwishkar, or by a Sraosha-varez, or by any priest, warrior, or husbandman.

19.
'But if there be in a Mazdean house a woman who is in her sickness, or a man who has become unfit for work, and who must sit in the place of infirmity, those clothes shall serve for their coverings and for their sheets, until they can withdraw their hands for prayer.

20.
'Ahura Mazda, indeed, does not allow us to waste anything of value that we may have, not even so much as an Asperena's weight of thread, not even so much as a maid lets fall in spinning.

21.
'Whosoever throws any clothing on a dead body, even so much as a maid lets fall in spinning, is not a pious man whilst alive, nor shall he, when dead, have a place in Paradise.

22.
'He makes himself a viaticum unto the world of the wicked, into that world, made of darkness, the offspring of darkness, which is Darkness' self. To that world, to the world of Hell, you are delivered by your own doings, by your own religion, O sinners!'

IV.
23.
O Maker of the material world, thou Holy One! Can he be clean again who has eaten of the carcass of a dog or of the corpse of a man?

24.
Ahura Mazda answered: 'He cannot, O holy Zarathushtra! His burrow shall be dug out, his heart shall be torn out, his bright

AVESTA: Vendidad

eyes shall be put out; the Druj Nasu falls upon him, takes hold of him even to the end of the nails, and he is unclean thenceforth, for ever and ever.'

V.
25.
O Maker of the material world, thou Holy One! Can he be clean again, O holy Ahura Mazda! who has brought a corpse with filth into the waters, or unto the fire, and made either unclean?
26.
Ahura Mazda answered: 'He cannot, O holy Zarathushtra! Those wicked ones it is, those Nasu-cutters, that most increase spiders and locusts; those wicked ones it is, those Nasu-cutters, that most increase the grass-destroying drought.
27. 'Those wicked ones it is, those Nasu-cutters, that increase most the power of the winter, produced by the fiends, the cattle-killing, thick- snowing, overflowing, the piercing, fierce, mischievous winter. Upon them comes and rushes the Druj Nasu she takes hold of them even to the end of the nails, and they are unclean, thenceforth, for ever and ever.'

VI.
28. O Maker of the material world, thou Holy One! Can the wood be made clean, O holy Ahura Mazda! whereunto Nasu has been brought from a dead dog, or from a dead man?
29. Ahura Mazda answered: 'It can, O holy Zarathushtra!'
How so?
'If the Nasu has not yet been expelled by the corpse-eating dogs, or by the corpse-eating birds, they shall lay down, apart on the ground, all the wood on a Vitasti a all around, if the wood be dry; on a Frarathni all around, if it be wet; then they shall sprinkle it once over with water, and it shall be clean.
30. 'But if the Nasu has already been expelled by the corpse-eating dogs, or by the corpse-eating birds, they shall lay down, apart

AVESTA: Vendidad

on the ground, all the wood on a Frarathni all around, if the wood be dry; on a Frabazu all around, if it be wet; then they shall sprinkle it once over with water, and it shall be clean.

31. 'Thus much of the wood around the dead shall they lay down, apart on the ground, according as the wood is dry or wet; as it is hard or soft; they shall sprinkle it once over with water, and it shall be clean.'

32. O Maker of the material world, thou Holy One! Can the corn or the fodder be made clean O holy Ahura Mazda! whereunto Nasu has been brought from a dead dog, or from a dead man?

33. Ahura Mazda answered: 'It can, O holy Zarathushtra!' How so?
'If the Nasu has not yet been expelled by the corpse-eating dogs, or by the corpse-eating birds they shall lay down, apart on the ground, all the corn on a Frarathni all around, if the corn be dry on a Frabazu all around, if it be wet; then they shall sprinkle it once over with water, and it shall be clean.

34. 'But if the Nasu has already been expelled by the corpse-eating dogs, or by the corpse-eating birds, they shall lay down, apart on the ground, all the corn on a Frabazu all around, if the corn be dry; on a Vibazu all around, if it be wet then they shall sprinkle it once over with water, and it shall be clean.

35. 'Thus much of the corn around the dead shall they lay down, apart on the ground, according as the corn is dry or wet; as it is sown or not sown; as it is reaped or not reaped; [as it is beaten or not beaten]1; as it is winnowed or not winnowed; [as it is ground or not ground]2; as it is kneaded [or not kneaded]3; they shall sprinkle it once over with water, and it shall be clean.'

VIIa.

36. O Maker of the material world, thou Holy One! If a worshipper of Mazda want to practice the art of healing, on whom shall he first prove his skill? on worshippers of Mazda or on worshippers of the Daevas?

37. Ahura Mazda answered: 'On worshippers of the Daevas shall

AVESTA: Vendidad

he first prove himself, rather than on worshippers of Mazda. If he treat with the knife a worshipper of the Daevas and he die; if he treat with the knife a second worshipper of the Daevas and he die; if he treat with the knife for the third time a worshipper of the Daevas and he die, he is unfit for ever and ever.

38. 'Let him therefore never attend any worshipper of Mazda; let him never treat with the knife and worshipper of Mazda, nor wound him with the knife. If he shall ever attend any worshipper of Mazda, if he shall ever treat with the knife any worshipper of Mazda, and wound him with the knife, he shall pay for his wound the penalty for willful murder.

39. 'If he treat with the knife a worshipper of the Daevas and he recover; if he treat with the knife a second worshipper of the Daevas and he recover; if for the third time he treat with the knife a worshipper of the Daevas and he recover; then he is fit for ever and ever.

40. 'He may henceforth at his will attend worshippers of Mazda; he may at his will treat with the knife worshippers of Mazda, and heal them with the knife.

VIIb.
41. 'A healer shall heal a priest for a blessing of the just; he shall heal the master of a house for the value of an ox of low value; he shall heal the lord of a borough for the value of an ox of average value; he shall heal the lord of a town for the value of an ox of high value; he shall heal the lord of a province for the value of a chariot and four.

42. 'He shall heal the wife of the master of a house for the value of a she-ass; he shall heal the wife of the lord of a borough for the value of a cow; he shall heal the wife of the lord of a town for the value of a mare; he shall heal the wife of the lord of a province for the value of a she-camel.

43. 'He shall heal the heir of a great house for the value of an ox of high value; he shall heal an ox of high value for the value of an ox of aver- age value; he shall heal an ox of

average value for the value of an ox of low value; he shall heal an ox of low value for the value of a sheep; he shall heal a sheep for the value of a piece of meat.

44. 'If several healers offer themselves together, O Spitama Zarathushtra! namely, one who heals with the knife, one who heals with herbs, and one who heals with the Holy Word, let one apply to the healing by the Holy Word: for this one is the best-healing of all healers who heals with the Holy Word; he will best drive away sickness from the body of the faithful.'

VIII.

45. O Maker of the material world, thou Holy One! How long after the corpse of a dead man has been laid down on the ground, clothed with the light of heaven and beholding the sun, is the ground clean again?

46. Ahura Mazda answered: 'When the corpse of a dead man has lain on the ground for a year, clothed with the light of heaven, and beholding the sun, then the ground is clean again, O holy Zarathushtra!'

47. O Maker of the material world, thou Holy One! How long after the corpse of a dead man has been buried in the earth, is the earth clean again?

48. Ahura Mazda answered: 'When the corpse of a dead man has lain buried in the earth for fifty years, O Spitama Zarathushtra! then the earth is clean again.'

49. O Maker of the material world, thou Holy One! How long after the corpse of a dead man has been laid down on a Dakhma, is the ground, whereon the Dakhma stands, clean again?

50. Ahura Mazda answered: 'Not until the dust of the corpse, O Spitama Zarathushtra! has mingled with the dust of the earth. Urge every one in the material world, O Spitama Zarathushtra! to pull down Dakhmas.

51. 'He who should pull down Dakhmas, even so much thereof as the size of his own body, his sins in thought, word, and deed are remitted as they would be by a Patet; his sins in thought,

AVESTA: Vendidad

word, and deed are undone.
52. 'Not for his soul shall the two spirits wage war with one another; and when he enters Paradise, the stars, the moon, and the sun shall rejoice in him; and I, Ahura Mazda, shall rejoice in him, saying: " Hail, O man! thou who hast just passed from the decaying world into the undecaying one!"'
55. O Maker of the material world, thou Holy One! Where are there Daevas: Where is it they offer worship to the Daevas: What is the place whereon troops of Daevas rush together, whereon troops of Daevas come rushing along? What is the place whereon they rush together to kill their fifties and their hundreds, their hundreds and their thousands, their thousands and their tens of thousands, their tens of thousands and their myriads of myriads?
56. Ahura Mazda answered: 'Those Dakhmas that are built upon the face of the earth, O Spitama Zarathushtra! and whereon are laid the corpses of dead men, that is the place where there are Daevas, that is the place whereon troops of Daevas rush together; whereon troops of Daevas come rushing along; whereon they rush together to kill their fifties and their hundreds, their hundreds and their thousands, their thousands and their tens of thousands, their tens of thousands and their myriads of myriads.
57. 'On those Dakhmas, O Spitama Zarathushtra! those Daevas take food and void filth. As you, men, in the material world, you cook meal and eat cooked meat, so do they. It is, as it were, the smell of their feeding that you smell there, O men!
58. 'For thus they go on reveling, until that stench is rooted in the Dakhmas. In those Dakhmas arise the infection of diseases, itch, hot fever, naeza, cold fever, rickets, and hair untimely white. On those Dakhmas meet the worst murderers, from the hour when the sun is down.
59. 'And people of small understanding who do not seek for better understanding, the Gainis make those diseases grow stronger by a third, on their thighs, on their hands, on their three-plaited hair.'

AVESTA: Vendidad

IX.

60. O Maker of the material world, thou Holy One! If in the house of a worshipper of Mazda there be a woman with child, and if being a month gone, or two, or three, or four, or five, or six, or seven, or eight, or nine, or ten months gone, she bring forth a still-born child, what shall the worshippers of Mazda do?

61. Ahura Mazda answered: 'The place in that Mazdean house whereof the ground is the cleanest and the driest, and the least passed through by flocks and herds, by the fire of Ahura Mazda, by the consecrated bundles of baresma, and by the faithful;'

62. O Maker of the material world, thou Holy One! How far from the fire? How far from the water? How far from the consecrated bundles of baresma? How far from the faithful?

63. Ahura Mazda answered: 'Thirty paces from the fire; thirty paces from the water; thirty paces from the consecrated bundles of Baresma; three paces from the faithful;—

64. 'On that place shall the worshippers of Mazda erect an enclosure, and therein shall they establish her with food, therein shall they establish her with clothes.'

65. O Maker of the material word, thou Holy One! What is the food that the woman shall first take?

66. Ahura Mazda answered: 'Gomez mixed with ashes, three draughts of it, or six, or nine, to send down the Dakhma within her womb.

67. 'Afterwards she may drink boiling milk of mares, cows, sheep, or goats, with pap or without pap; she may take cooked milk without water, meal without water, and wine without water.'

68. O Maker of the material world, thou Holy One! How long shall she remain so? How long shall she live thus on milk, meal, and wine?

69. Ahura Mazda answered: 'Three nights long shall she remain so; three nights long shall she live thus on milk, meal, and wine. Then, when three nights have passed, she shall wash her body, she shall wash her clothes, with gomez and water, by the nine holes, and thus shall she be clean.'

70. O Maker of the material world, thou Holy One! But if fever

AVESTA: Vendidad

befall her unclean body, if these two worst pains, hunger and
thirst, befall her, may she be allowed to drink water?
71. Ahura Mazda answered: 'She may; the first thing for her
is to have her life saved. From the hands of one of the holy men,
a holy faithful man, who knows the holy knowledge, she shall drink
of the strength-giving water. But you, worshippers of Mazda, fix
ye the penalty for it. The Ratu being applied to, the Sraosha-varez
being applied to, shall prescribe the penalty to be paid.'
72. What is the penalty to be paid?
Ahura Mazda answered: 'The deed is that of a Peshotanu: two
hundred stripes with the Aspahe-astra, two hundred stripes with
the Sraosho-charana.'

X.
73. O Maker of the material world, thou Holy One! Can the
eating-vessels be made clean that have been touched by Nasu from
a dog, or Nasu from a man?
74. Ahura Mazda answered: 'They can, O holy Zarathushtra!'
How so?
'If they be of gold, you shall wash them once with gomez,
you shall rub them once with earth, you shall wash them once with
water, and they shall be clean.
'If they be of silver, you shall wash them twice with gomez,
you shall rub them twice with earth, you shall wash them twice
with water, and they shall be clean.
[75. 'If they be of brass, you shall wash them thrice with
gomez, you shall rub them thrice with earth, you shall wash them
thrice with water, and they shall be clean.
'If they be of steel, you shall wash them four times with
gomez, you shall rub them four times with earth, you shall wash
them four times with water, and they shall be clean.
'If they be of stone, you shall wash them six times with gomez,
you shall rub them six times with earth, you shall wash them six
times with water, and they shall be clean.]
'If they be of earth, of wood, or of clay, they are unclean

AVESTA: Vendidad

for ever and ever.'

XI.
76. O Maker of the material world, thou Holy One! Can the cow be made clean that has eaten of the carcass of a dog, or of the corpse of a man?
77. Ahura Mazda answered: 'She can, O holy Zarathushtra! The priest shall not, within a year, take from her either milk or cheese for the libation, nor meat for the libation and the Baresma. When a year has passed, then the faithful may eat of her as before.'

XII.
78. Who is he, O holy Ahura Mazda! who, meaning well and desiring righteousness, prevents righteousness? Who is he who, meaning well, falls into the ways of the Druj?
79. Ahura Mazda answered: 'This one, meaning well and desiring righteousness, prevents righteousness; this one, meaning well, falls into the ways of the Druj, who offers up water defiled by the dead and unfit for libation; or who offers up in the dead of the night water unfit for libation.'

FARGARD 8. Purity laws

I.
1.
If a dog or a man die under a hut of wood or a hut of felt, what shall the worshippers of Mazda do?
2.
Ahura Mazda answered: 'They shall search for a Dakhma, they shall look for a Dakhma all around. If they find it easier to

AVESTA: Vendidad

remove the dead, they shall take out the dead, they shall let
the house stand, and shall perfume it with Urvasna or Vohu–gaona,
or Vohu–kereti, or Hadha–naepata, or any other sweet–smelling
plant.

3.
'If they find it easier to remove the house, they shall take
away the house, they shall let the dead he on the spot, and shall
perfume the house with Urvasna, or Vohu–gaona, or Vohu–kereti,
or Hadha–naepata, or any other sweet–smelling plant.'

II
4.
O Maker of the material world, thou Holy One! If in the house
of a worshipper of Mazda a dog or a man happens to die, and it
is raining, or snowing, or blowing, or it is dark, or the day
is at its end, when flocks and men lose their way, what shall
the worshippers of Mazda do?

5.
Ahura Mazda answered: 'The place in that house whereof the
ground is the cleanest and the driest, and the least passed through
by flocks and herds, by the fire of Ahura Mazda, by the consecrated
bundles of Baresma, and by the faithful;'–

6.
O Maker of the material world, thou Holy One! How far from
the fire? How far from the water? How far from the consecrated
bundles of Baresma? How far from the faithful?

7.
Ahura Mazda answered: 'Thirty paces from the fire; thirty
paces from the water; thirty paces from the consecrated bundles
of Baresma; three paces from the faithful;–

8.
'On that place they shall dig a grave, half a foot deep if
the earth be hard, half the height of a man if it be soft; [they
shall cover the surface of the grave with ashes or cowdung]; they
shall cover the surface of it with dust of bricks, of stones,

AVESTA: Vendidad

or of dry earth.

9.

'And they shall let the lifeless body lie there, for two nights,
or three nights, or a month long, until the birds begin to fly,
the plants to grow, the hidden floods to flow, and the wind to
dry up the earth.

10.

'And when the birds begin to fly, the plants to grow, the
hidden floods to flow, and the wind to dry up the earth, then
the worshippers of Mazda shall make a breach in the wall of the
house, and two men, strong and skillful, having stripped their
clothes off, shall take up the body from the clay or the stones,
or from the plastered house, and they shall lay it down on a place
where they know there are always corpse-eating dogs and corpse-eating
birds.

11.

'Afterwards the corpse-bearers shall sit down, three paces
from the dead, and the holy Ratu shall proclaim to the worshippers
of Mazda thus: "Worshippers of Mazda, let the urine be brought
here wherewith the corpse-bearers there shall wash their hair
and their bodies!"'

12.

O Maker of the material world, thou Holy One! Which is the
urine wherewith the corpse-bearers shall wash their hair and their
bodies? Is it of sheep or of oxen? Is it of man or of woman?

13.

Ahura Mazda answered: 'It is of sheep or of oxen; not of man
nor of woman, except a man or a woman who has married the next-of-kin:
these shall therefore procure the urine wherewith the corpse-bearers
shall wash their hair and their bodies.'

III

14.

O Maker of the material world, thou Holy One! Can the way,
whereon the carcasses of dogs or corpses of men have been carried,

AVESTA: Vendidad

be passed through again by flocks and herds, by men and women,
by the fire of Ahura Mazda, by the consecrated bundles of Baresma,
and by the faithful?
15.
Ahura Mazda answered: 'It cannot be passed through again by
flocks and herds, nor by men and women, nor by the fire of Ahura
Mazda, nor by the consecrated bundles of Baresma, nor by the faithful.
16.
'They shall therefore cause a yellow dog with four eyes, or
a white dog with yellow ears, to go three times through that way.
When either the yellow dog with four eyes, or the white dog with
yellow ears, is brought there, then the Druj Nasu flies away to
the regions of the north, [in the shape of a raging fly, with
knees and tail sticking out, droning without end, and like unto
the foulest Khrafstras.]
17.
'If the dog goes unwillingly, O Spitama Zarathushtra, they
shall cause the yellow dog with four eyes, or the white dog with
yellow ears, to go six times through that way. When either the
yellow dog with four eyes, or the white dog with yellow ears,
is brought there, then the Druj Nasu flies away to the regions
of the north, [in the shape of a raging fly, with knees and tail
sticking out, droning without end, and like unto the foulest Khrafstras.]
18.
'If the dog goes unwillingly, they shall cause the yellow
dog with four eyes, or the white dog with yellow ears, to go nine
times through that way. When either the yellow dog with four eyes,
or the white dog with yellow ears, has been brought there, then
the Druj Nasu flies away to the regions of the north, [in the
shape of a raging fly, with knees and tail sticking out, droning
without end, and like unto the foulest Khrafstras.]
19.
'An Athravan shall first go along the way and shall say aloud
these victorious words: "Yatha aha vairyo: – The will of
the Lord is the law of righteousness.
"'The gifts of Vohu–mano to the deeds done in this world

AVESTA: Vendidad

for Mazda.
"'He who relieves the poor makes Ahura king.
20.
"'Kem–na mazda: – What protector hast thou given unto
me, O Mazda! while the hate of the wicked encompasses me? Whom
but thy Atar and Vohu–mano, through whose work I keep on the world
of righteousness? Reveal therefore to me thy Religion as thy rule!

"'Ke verethrem–ja: – Who is the victorious who will protect
thy teaching? Make it clear that I am the guide for both worlds.
May Sraosha come with Vohu–mano and help whomsoever thou pleasest,
O Mazda!
21.
"'Keep us from our hater, O Mazda and Armaiti Spenta!
Perish, O fiendish Druj! Perish, O brood of the fiend! Perish,
O creation of the fiend! Perish, O world of the fiend! Perish
away, O Druj! Rush away, O Druj! Perish away, O Druj! Perish away
to the regions of the north, never more to give unto death the
living world of Righteousness!"
22.
'Then the worshippers of Mazda may at their will bring by
those ways sheep and oxen, men and women, and Fire, the son of
Ahura Mazda, the consecrated bundles of Baresma, and the faithful.

'The worshippers of Mazda may afterwards prepare meals with meat
and wine in that house; it shall be clean, and there will be no
sin, as before.'

IV
23.
O Maker of the material world, thou Holy One! If a man shall
throw clothes, either of skin or woven, upon a dead body, enough
to cover the feet, what is the penalty that he shall pay? Ahura
Mazda answered: 'Four hundred stripes with the Aspahe–astra, four
hundred stripes with the Sraosho–charana.'

AVESTA: Vendidad

24.
O Maker of the material world, thou Holy One! If a man shall throw clothes, either of skin or woven, upon a dead body, enough to cover both legs, what is the penalty that he shall pay? Ahura Mazda answered: 'Six hundred stripes with the Aspahe–astra, six hundred stripes with the Sraosho–charana.'

25.
O Maker of the material world, thou Holy One! If a man shall throw clothes, either of skin or woven, upon a dead body, enough to cover the whole body, what is the penalty that he shall pay? Ahura Mazda answered: 'A thousand stripes with the Aspahe–astra, a thousand stripes with the Sraosho–charana.'

V

26.
O Maker of the material world, thou Holy One! If a man, by force, commits the unnatural sin, what is the penalty that he shall pay?
Ahura Mazda answered: 'Eight hundred stripes with the Aspahe–astra, eight hundred stripes with the Sraosho–charana.'

27.
O Maker of the material world, thou Holy One! If a man voluntarily commits the unnatural sin, what is the penalty for it? What is the atonement for it? What is the cleansing from it?
Ahura Mazda answered: 'For that deed there is nothing that can pay, nothing that can atone, nothing that can cleanse from it; it is a trespass for which there is no atonement, for ever and ever.'

28.
When is it so?
'It is so if the sinner be a professor of the Religion of Mazda, or one who has been taught in it.
'But if he be not a professor of the Religion of Mazda, nor one who has been taught in it, then his sin is taken from him, if he makes confession of the Religion of Mazda and resolves never

AVESTA: Vendidad

to commit again such forbidden deeds.

29.
'The Religion of Mazda indeed, O Spitama Zarathushtra! takes away from him who makes confession of it the bonds of his sin; it takes away (the sin of) breach of trust; it takes away (the sin of) murdering one of the faithful; it takes away (the sin of) burying a corpse; it takes away (the sin of) deeds for which there is no atonement; it takes away the worst sin of usury; it takes away any sin that may be sinned.

30.
In the same way the Religion of Mazda, O Spitama Zarathushtra! cleanses the faithful from every evil thought, word, and deed, as a swift-rushing mighty wind cleanses the plain.
'So let all the deeds he doeth be henceforth good, O Zarathushtra! a full atonement for his sin is effected by means of the Religion of Mazda.'

31.
O Maker of the material world, thou Holy One! Who is the man that is a Daeva? Who is he that is a worshipper of the Daevas? that is a male paramour of the Daevas? that is a female paramour of the Daevas? that is a wife to the Daeva? that is as bad as a Daeva: that is in his whole being a Daeva? Who is he that is a Daeva before he dies, and becomes one of the unseen Daevas after death?

32.
Ahura Mazda answered: 'The man that lies with mankind as man lies with womankind, or as woman lies with mankind, is the man that is a Daeva; this one is the man that is a worshipper of the Daevas, that is a male paramour of the Daevas, that is a female paramour of the Daevas, that is a wife to the Daeva; this is the man that is as bad as a Daeva, that is in his whole being a Daeva; this is the man that is a Daeva before he dies, and becomes one of the unseen Daevas after death: so is he, whether he has lain with mankind as mankind, or as womankind.'

AVESTA: Vendidad

VI

33.
O Maker of the material world, thou Holy One! Shall the man be clean who has touched a corpse that has been dried up and dead more than a year?

34.
Ahura Mazda answered: 'He shall. The dry mingles not with the dry. Should the dry mingle with the dry, how soon all this material world of mine would be only one Peshotanu, bent on the destruction of righteousness, and whose soul will cry and wail! so numberless are the beings that die upon the face of the earth.'

VII

35.
O Maker of the material world, thou Holy One! Can the man be made clean that has touched the corpse of a dog or the corpse of a man?

36.
Ahura Mazda answered: 'He can, O holy Zarathushtra!'
How so?
'If the Nasu has already been expelled by the corpse-eating dogs, or by the corpse-eating birds, he shall cleanse his body with gomez and water, and he shall be clean.

37.
'If the Nasu has not yet been expelled by the corpse-eating dogs, or by the corpse-eating birds, then the worshippers of Mazda shall dig three holes in the ground, and he shall thereupon wash his body with gomez, not with water. They shall then lift and bring my dog, they shall bring him (thus shall it be done and not otherwise) in front [of the man].

38.
'The worshippers of Mazda shall dig three other holes in the ground, and he shall thereupon wash his body with gomez, not with water. They shall then lift and bring my dog, they shall bring him (thus shall it be done and not otherwise) in front [of the

man]. Then shall they wait until he is dried even to the last hair on the top of his head.

39.

'They shall dig three more holes in the ground, three paces away from the preceding, and he shall thereupon wash his body with water, not with gomez.

40.

'He shall first wash his hands; if his hands be not first washed, he makes the whole of his body unclean. When he has washed his hands three times, after his hands have been washed, thou shalt sprinkle with water the forepart of his skull.'

41.

O Maker of the material world, thou Holy One! When the good waters reach the forepart of the skull, whereon does the Druj Nasu rush?

Ahura Mazda answered: 'In front, between the brows, the Druj Nasu rushes.'

42.

O Maker of the material world, thou Holy One! When the good waters reach in front, between the brows, whereon does the Druj Nasu rush?

Ahura Mazda answered: 'On the back part of the skull the Druj Nasu rushes.'

43.

O Maker of the material world, thou Holy One! When the good waters reach the back part of the skull, whereon does the Druj Nasu rush?

Ahura Mazda answered: 'In front, on the jaws, the Druj Nasu rushes.'

44.

O Maker of the material world, thou Holy One! When the good waters reach in front, on the jaws, whereon does the Druj Nasu rush?

Ahura Mazda answered: 'Upon the right ear the Druj Nasu rushes.'

45.

O Maker of the material world, thou Holy One! When the good waters reach the right ear, whereon does the Druj Nasu rush?

AVESTA: Vendidad

Ahura Mazda answered: 'Upon the left ear the Druj Nasu rushes.'
46.
O Maker of the material world, thou Holy One! When the good waters reach the left ear, whereon does the Druj Nasu rush?
Ahura Mazda answered: 'Upon the right shoulder the Druj Nasu rushes.'
47.
O Maker of the material world, thou Holy One! When the good waters reach the right shoulder, whereon does the Druj Nasu rush?

Ahura Mazda answered: 'Upon the left shoulder the Druj Nasu rushes.'
48.
O Maker of the material world, thou Holy One! When the good waters reach the left shoulder, whereon does the Druj Nasu rush?

Ahura Mazda answered: 'Upon the right arm-pit the Druj Nasu rushes.'
49.
O Maker of the material world, thou Holy One! When the good waters reach the right arm-pit, whereon does the Druj Nasu rush?

Ahura Mazda answered: 'Upon the left arm-pit the Druj Nasu rushes.'
50.
O Maker of the material world, thou Holy One! When the good waters reach the left arm-pit, whereon does the Druj Nasu rush?

Ahura Mazda answered: 'In front, upon the chest, the Druj Nasu rushes.'
51.
O Maker of the material world, thou Holy One! When the good waters reach the chest in front, whereon does the Druj Nasu rush?

Ahura Mazda answered: 'Upon the back the Druj Nasu rushes.'
52.
O Maker of the material world, thou Holy One! When the good waters reach the back, whereon does the Druj Nasu rush?
Ahura Mazda answered: 'Upon the right nipple the Druj Nasu rushes.'
53.

AVESTA: Vendidad

O Maker of the material world, thou Holy One! When the good waters reach the right nipple, whereon does the Druj Nasu rush? Ahura Mazda answered: 'Upon the left nipple the Druj Nasu rushes.'
54.
O Maker of the material world, thou Holy One! When the good waters reach the left nipple, whereon does the Druj Nasu rush? Ahura Mazda answered: 'Upon the right rib the Druj Nasu rushes.'
55.
O Maker of the material world, thou Holy One! When the good waters reach the right rib, whereon does the Druj Nasu rush? Ahura Mazda answered: 'Upon the left rib the Druj Nasu rushes.'
56.
O Maker of the material world, thou Holy One! When the good waters reach the left rib, whereon does the Druj Nasu rush? Ahura Mazda answered: 'Upon the right hip the Druj Nasu rushes.'
57.
O Maker of the material world, thou Holy One! When the good waters reach the right hip, whereon does the Druj Nasu rush? Ahura Mazda answered: 'Upon the left hip the Druj Nasu rushes.'
58.
O Maker of the material world, thou Holy One! When the good waters reach the left hip, whereon does the Druj Nasu rush? Ahura Mazda answered: 'Upon the sexual parts the Druj Nasu rushes. If the unclean one be a man, thou shalt sprinkle him first behind, then before; if the unclean one be a woman, thou shalt sprinkle her first before, then behind.'
59.
O Maker of the material world, thou Holy One! When the good waters reach the sexual parts, whereon does the Druj Nasu rush?

Ahura Mazda answered: 'Upon the right thigh the Druj Nasu rushes.'
60.
O Maker of the material world, thou Holy One! When the good waters reach the right thigh, whereon does the Druj Nasu rush? Ahura Mazda answered: 'Upon the left thigh the Druj Nasu rushes.'
61.

AVESTA: Vendidad

O Maker of the material world, thou Holy One! When the good waters reach the left thigh, whereon does the Druj Nasu rush?
Ahura Mazda answered: 'Upon the right knee the Druj Nasu rushes.'
62.
O Maker of the material world, thou Holy One! When the good waters reach the right knee, whereon does the Druj Nasu rush?
Ahura Mazda answered: 'Upon the left knee the Druj Nasu rushes.'
63.
O Maker of the material world, thou Holy One! When the good waters reach the left knee, whereon does the Druj Nasu rush?
Ahura Mazda answered: 'Upon the right leg the Druj Nasu rushes.'
64.
O Maker of the material world, thou Holy One! When the good waters reach the right leg, whereon does the Druj Nasu rush?
Ahura Mazda answered: 'Upon the left leg the Druj Nasu rushes.'
65.
O Maker of the material world, thou Holy One! When the good waters reach the left leg, whereon does the Druj Nasu rush?
Ahura Mazda answered: 'Upon the right ankle the Druj Nasu rushes.'
66.
O Maker of the material world, thou Holy One! When the good waters reach the right ankle, whereon does the Druj Nasu rush?
Ahura Mazda answered: 'Upon the left ankle the Druj Nasu rushes.'
67.
O Maker of the material world, thou Holy One! When the good waters reach the left ankle, whereon does the Druj Nasu rush?
Ahura Mazda answered: 'Upon the right instep the Druj Nasu rushes.'
68.
O Maker of the material world, thou Holy One! When the good waters reach the right instep, whereon does the Druj Nasu rush?
Ahura Mazda answered: 'Upon the left instep the Druj Nasu rushes.'
69.
O Maker of the material world, thou Holy One! When the good waters reach the left instep, whereon does the Druj Nasu rush?
Ahura Mazda answered: 'She turns round under the sole of the foot; it looks like the wing of a fly.

AVESTA: Vendidad

70.
'He shall press his toes upon the ground, and shall raise up his heels; thou shalt sprinkle his right sole with water; then the Druj Nasu rushes upon the left sole. Thou shalt sprinkle the left sole with water; then the Druj Nasu turns round under the toes; it looks like the wing of a fly.

71.
'He shall press his heels upon the ground, and shall raise up his toes; thou shalt sprinkle his right toe with water; then the Druj Nasu rushes upon the left toe. Thou shalt sprinkle the left toe with water; then the Druj Nasu flies away to the regions of the north, in the shape of a raging fly, with knees and tail sticking out, droning without end, and like unto the foulest Khrafstras.
[
72.
'And thou shalt say aloud these victorious, most healing words:

'"The will of the Lord is the law of holiness," etc.

'"What protector hast thou given unto me, O Mazda! while the hate of the wicked encompasses me?"
'"Who is the victorious who will protect thy teaching?"

'"Keep us from our hater, O Mazda and Armaiti Spenta! Perish, O fiendish Druj! Perish, O brood of the fiend! Perish,

O creation of the fiend! Perish O world of the fiend! Perish away, O Druj! Rush away, O Druj! Perish away, O Druj! Perish away to the regions of the north, never more to give unto death the living world of Righteousness!"']

VIII
73.
O Maker of the material world, thou Holy One! If worshippers of Mazda, walking, or running, or riding, or driving, come upon

AVESTA: Vendidad

a Nasu-burning fire, whereon Nasu is being burnt or cooked, what shall they do?

74.
Ahura Mazda answered: 'They shall kill the man that cooks the Nasu; surely they shall kill him. They shall take off the cauldron, they shall take off the tripod.

75.
'Then they shall kindle wood from that fire; either wood of those trees that have the seed of fire in them, or bundles of the very wood that was prepared for that fire; then they shall take it farther and disperse it, that it may die out the sooner.

76.
'Thus they shall lay a first bundle on the ground, a Vitasti away from the Nasu-burning fire; then they shall take it farther and disperse it, that it may die out the sooner.

77.
'They shall lay down a second bundle on the ground, a Vitasti away from the Nasu-burning fire: then they shall take it farther and disperse it, that it may die out the sooner.

'They shall lay down a third bundle on the ground, a Vitasti away from the Nasu-burning fire; then they shall take it farther and disperse it, that it may die out the sooner.

'They shall lay down a fourth bundle on the ground, a Vitasti away from the Nasu-burning fire; then they shall take it farther and disperse it, that it may die out the sooner.

'They shall lay down a fifth bundle on the ground, a Vitasti away from the Nasu-burning fire; then they shall take it farther and disperse it, that it may die out the sooner.

'They shall lay down a sixth bundle on the ground, a Vitasti away from the Nasu-burning fire; then they shall take it farther and disperse it, that it may die out the sooner.

'They shall lay down a seventh bundle on the ground, a Vitasti away from the Nasu-burning fire; then they shall take it farther and disperse it, that it may die out the sooner.

They shall lay down an eighth bundle on the ground, a Vitasti away from the Nasu-burning fire; then they shall take it farther

AVESTA: Vendidad

and disperse it, that it may die out the sooner.
78.
'They shall lay down a ninth bundle on the ground, a Vitasti away from the Nasu-burning fire; then they shall take it farther and disperse it, that it may die out the sooner.
79.
'If a man shall then piously bring unto the fire, O Spitama Zarathushtra! wood of Urvasna, or Vohu-gaona, or Vohu-kereti, or Hadha-naepata, or any other sweet-smelling wood;
80.
'Wheresoever the wind shall bring the perfume of the fire, thereunto the fire of Ahura Mazda shall go and kill thousands of unseen Daevas, thousands of fiends, the brood of darkness, thousands of couples of Yatus and Pairikas.'

IX
81.
O Maker of the material world, thou Holy One! If a man bring a Nasu-burning fire to the Daityo-gatu, what shall be his reward when his soul has parted with his body?
Ahura Mazda answered: 'His reward shall be the same as if he had, here below, brought ten thousand fire-brands to the Daityo-gatu.'
82.
O Maker of the material world, thou Holy One! If a man bring to the Daityo-gatu the fire wherein impure liquid has been burnt, what shall be his reward when his soul has parted with his body?

Ahura Mazda answered: 'His reward shall be the same as if he had, here below, brought a thousand fire-brands to the Daityo-gatu.
83.
O Maker of the material world, thou Holy One! If a man bring to the Daityo-gatu the fire wherein dung has been burnt, what shall be his reward when his soul has parted with his body?
Ahura Mazda answered: 'His reward shall be the same as if he had, here below, brought five hundred fire-brands to the Daityo-gatu.'

AVESTA: Vendidad

84.
O Maker of the material world, thou Holy One! If a man bring to the Daityo-gatu the fire from the kiln of a potter, what shall be his reward when his soul has parted with his body?
Ahura Mazda answered: 'His reward shall be the same as if he had, here below, brought four hundred fire-brands to the Daityo-gatu.'
85.
O Maker of the material world, thou Holy One! If a man bring to the Daityo-gatu the fire from a glazier's kiln, what shall be his reward when his soul has parted with his body?
Ahura Mazda answered: 'His reward shall be the same as if he had, here below, brought to the Daityo-gatu as many fire-brands as there were glasses [brought to that fire].'
86.
O Maker of the material world, thou Holy One! If a man bring to the Daityo-gatu the fire from the aonya paro-berejya, what shall be his reward when his soul has parted with his body?
Ahura Mazda answered: 'His reward shall be the same as if he had, here below, brought to the Daityo-gatu as many fire-brands as there were plants.'
87.
O Maker of the material world, thou Holy One! If a man bring to the Daityo-gatu the fire from under the puncheon of a goldsmith, what shall be his reward when his soul has parted with his body?

Ahura Mazda answered: 'His reward shall be the same as if he had, here below, brought a hundred fire-brands to the Daityo-gatu.'
88.
O Maker of the material world, thou Holy One! If a man bring to the Daityo-gatu the fire from under the puncheon of a silversmith, what shall be his reward when his soul has parted with his body?

Ahura Mazda answered: 'His reward shall be the same as if he had, here below, brought ninety fire-brands to the Daityo-gatu.'
89.
O Maker of the material world, thou Holy One! If a man bring

AVESTA: Vendidad

to the Daityo-gatu the fire from under the puncheon of a blacksmith, what shall be his reward when his soul has parted with his body?

Ahura Mazda answered: 'His reward shall be the same as if he had, here below, brought eighty fire-brands to the Daityo-gatu.'
90.
O Maker of the material world, thou Holy One! It a man bring to the Daityo-gatu the fire from under the puncheon of a worker in steel, what shall be his reward when his soul has parted with his body?
Ahura Mazda answered: 'His reward shall be the same as if he had, here below, brought seventy fire-brands to the Daityo-gatu.'
91.
O Maker of the material world, thou Holy One! If a man bring to the Daityo-gatu the fire of an oven, what shall be his reward when his soul has parted from his body?
Ahura Mazda answered: 'His reward shall be the same as if he had, here below, brought sixty fire-brands to the Daityo-gatu.'
92.
O Maker of the material world, thou Holy One! If a man bring to the Daityo-gatu the fire from under a cauldron, what shall be his reward when his soul has parted with his body?
Ahura Mazda answered: 'His reward shall be the same as it he had, here below, brought fifty fire-brands to the Daityo-gatu.'
93.
O Maker of the material world, thou Holy One! If a man bring to the Daityo-gatu the fire from an aonya takhairya, what shall be his reward when his soul has parted with his body?
Ahura Mazda answered: 'His reward shall be the same as if he had, here below, brought forty fire-brands to the Daityo-gatu.'
94.
O Maker of the material world, thou Holy One! If a man bring a herdsman's fire to the Daityo-gatu, what shall be his reward when his soul has parted with his body?
Ahura Mazda answered: 'His reward shall be the same as if he had, here below, brought thirty fire-brands to the Daityo-gatu.'

AVESTA: Vendidad

95.
O Maker of the material world, thou Holy One! If a man bring to the Daityo-gatu the fire of the field, what shall be his reward when his soul has parted with his body?
Ahura Mazda answered: 'His reward shall be the same as if he had, here below, brought twenty fire-brands to the Daityo-gatu.']
96.
O Maker of the material world, thou Holy One! If a man bring to the Daityo-gatu the fire of his own hearth, what shall be his reward when his soul has parted with his body?
Ahura Mazda answered: 'His reward shall be the same as if he had, here below, brought ten fire-brands to the Daityo-gatu.'

X
97.
O Maker of the material world, thou Holy One! Can a man be made clean, O holy Ahura Mazda! who has touched a corpse in a distant place in the wilderness?
98.
Ahura Mazda answered: 'He can, O holy Zarathushtra.'
How so?
'If the Nasu has already been expelled by the corpse-eating dogs or the corpse-eating birds, he shall wash his body with gomez; he shall wash it thirty times, he shall rub it dry with the hand thirty times, beginning every time with the head.
99.
'If the Nasu has not yet been expelled by the corpse-eating dogs or the corpse-eating birds, he shall wash his body with gomez; he shall wash it fifteen times, he shall rub it dry with the hand fifteen times.
100.
'Then he shall run a distance of a Hathra. He shall run until he meets some man on his way, and he shall cry out aloud: "Here am I, one who has touched the corpse of a man, and who is powerless in mind, powerless in tongue, powerless in hand. Do make me clean."

AVESTA: Vendidad

Thus shall he run until he overtakes the man. If the man will
not cleanse him, he remits him the third of his trespass.
101.
'Then he shall run another Hathra, he shall run off again
until he overtakes a man; if the man will not cleanse him, he
remits him the half of his trespass.
102.
'Then he shall run a third Hathra, he shall run off a third
time until he overtakes a man; if the man will not cleanse him,
he remits him the whole of his trespass.
103.
'Thus shall he run forwards until he comes near a house, a
borough, a town, an inhabited district, and he shall cry out with
a loud voice: "Here am I, one who has touched the corpse
of a man, and who is powerless in mind, powerless in tongue, powerless
in hand. Do make me clean." If they will not cleanse him,
he shall cleanse his body with gomez and water; thus shall he
be clean.'
104.
O Maker of the material world, thou Holy One! If he find water
on his way and the water make him subject to a penalty, what is
the penalty that he shall pay?
105.
Ahura Mazda answered: 'Four hundred stripes with the Aspahe–astra,
four hundred stripes with the Sraosho–charana.'
106.
O Maker of the material world, thou Holy One! If he find trees
on his way and the fire make him subject to a penalty, what is
the penalty that he shall pay?
Ahura Mazda answered: 'Four hundred stripes with the Aspahe–astra,
four hundred stripes with the Sraosho–charana.
107.
'This is the penalty, this is the atonement which saves the
faithful man who submits to it, not him who does not submit to
it.
Such a one shall surely be an inhabitant in the mansion of the

AVESTA: Vendidad

Druj.'

FARGARD 9. The Nine Nights' Barashnum.

Ia.
1.
Zarathushtra asked Ahura Mazda: O most beneficent Spirit, Maker of the material world, thou Holy One! To whom shall they apply here below, who want to cleanse their body defiled by the dead?'
2.
Ahura Mazda answered: 'To a pious man, O Spitama Zarathushtra! who knows how to speak, who speaks truth, who has learned the Holy Word, who is pious, and knows best the rites of cleansing according to the law of Mazda. That man shall fell the trees off the surface of the ground on a space of nine Vibazus square;
3.
'in that part of the ground where there is least water and where there are fewest trees, the part which is the cleanest and driest, and the least passed through by sheep and oxen, and by the fire of Ahura Mazda, by the consecrated bundles of Baresma, and by the faithful.'
4.
How far from the fire? How far from the water? How far from the consecrated bundles of Baresma? How far from the faithful?
5.
Ahura Mazda answered: 'Thirty paces from the fire, thirty paces from the water, thirty paces from the consecrated bundles of Baresma, three paces from the faithful.
6.
'Then thou shalt dig a hole, two fingers deep if the summer has come, four fingers deep if the winter and ice have come.

AVESTA: Vendidad

7.
'Thou shalt dig a second hole, two fingers deep if the summer has come, four fingers deep if the winter end ice have come.
'Thou shalt dig a third hole, two fingers deep if the summer has come, four fingers deep if the winter and ice have come.
'Thou shalt dig a fourth hole, two fingers deep if the summer has come, four fingers deep if the winter and ice have come.
'Thou shalt dig a fifth hole, two fingers deep if the summer has come, four fingers deep if the winter and ice have come.
'Thou shalt dig a sixth hole, two fingers deep if the summer has come, four fingers deep if the winter and ice have come.'

8.
How far from one another?
'One pace.'
How much is the pace?
'As much as three feet.

9.
'Then thou shalt dig three holes more, two fingers deep if the summer has come, four fingers deep if the winter and ice have come.'
How far from the former six?
'Three paces.'
What sort of paces?
'Such as are taken in walking.'
How much are those (three) paces?
'As much as nine feet.

10.
'Then thou shalt draw a furrow all around with a metal knife.'

How far from the holes?
'Three paces.'
What sort of paces?
'Such as are taken in walking.'
How much are those (three) paces?
'As much as nine feet.

11.

AVESTA: Vendidad

'Then thou shalt draw twelve furrows; three of which thou shalt draw to surround and divided [from the rest] (the first) three holes; three thou shalt draw to surround and divide (the first) six holes; three thou shalt draw to surround and divide the nine holes; three thou shalt draw around the [three] inferior holes, outside the [six other] holes. At each of the three times nine feet, thou shalt place stones as steps to the holes; or potsherds, or stumps, or clods, or any hard matter.'

Ib.
12.
'Then the man defiled shall walk to the holes; thou, O Zarathushtra! shalt stand outside by the furrow, and thou shalt recite, Nemascha ya armaitish izhacha; and the man defiled shall repeat, Nemascha ya armaitish izhacha.
13.
'The Druj becomes weaker and weaker at every one of those words which are a weapon to smite the fiend Angra Mainyu, to smite Aeshma of the murderous spear, to smite the Mazainya fiends, to smite all the fiends.
14.
'Then thou shalt take for the gomez a spoon of brass or of lead. When thou takest a stick with nine knots, O Spitama Zarathushtra! to sprinkle (the gomez) from that spoon, thou shalt fasten the spoon to the end of the stick.
15.
'They shall wash his hands first. If his hands be not washed first, he makes his whole body unclean. When he has washed his hands three times, after his hands have been washed, thou shalt sprinkle the forepart of his skull; then the Druj Nasu rushes in front, between his brows.
16.
Thou shalt sprinkle him in front between the brows; then the Druj Nasu rushes upon the back part of the skull.
'Thou shalt sprinkle the back part of the skull; then the Druj

AVESTA: Vendidad

Nasu rushes upon the jaws.
'Thou shalt sprinkle the jaws; then the Druj Nasu rushes upon the right ear.

17.
'Thou shalt sprinkle the right ear; then the Druj Nasu rushes upon the left ear.
'Thou shalt sprinkle the left ear; then the Druj Nasu rushes upon the right shoulder.
'Thou shalt sprinkle the right shoulder; then the Druj Nasu rushes upon the left shoulder.
'Thou shalt sprinkle the left shoulder; then the Druj Nasu rushes upon the right arm-pit.

18.
'Thou shalt sprinkle the right arm-pit; then the Druj Nasu rushes upon the left arm-pit.
'Thou shalt sprinkle the left arm-pit; then the Druj Nasu rushes upon the chest.
'Thou shalt sprinkle the chest; then the Druj Nasu rushes upon the back.

19.
'Thou shalt sprinkle the back; then the Druj Nasu rushes upon the right nipple.
'Thou shalt sprinkle the right nipple; then the Druj Nasu rushes upon the left nipple.
'Thou shalt sprinkle the left nipple; then the Druj Nasu rushes upon the right rib.

20.
'Thou shalt sprinkle the right rib; then the Druj Nasu rushes upon the left rib.
'Thou shalt sprinkle the left rib; then the Druj Nasu rushes upon the right hip.
'Thou shalt sprinkle the right hip; then the Druj Nasu rushes 'upon the left hip.

21.
'Thou shalt sprinkle the left hip; then the Druj Nasu rushes upon the sexual parts.

AVESTA: Vendidad

'Thou shalt sprinkle the sexual parts. If the unclean one be a man, thou shalt sprinkle him first behind, then before; if the unclean one be a woman, thou shalt sprinkle her first before, then behind; then the Druj Nasu rushes upon the right thigh.

22.
'Thou shalt sprinkle the right thigh; then the Druj Nasu rushes upon the left thigh.
'Thou shalt sprinkle the left thigh; then the Druj Nasu rushes upon the right knee.
'Thou shalt sprinkle the right knee; then the Druj Nasu rushes upon the left knee.

23.
'Thou shalt sprinkle the left knee; then the Druj Nasu rushes upon the right leg.
'Thou shalt sprinkle the right leg; then the Druj Nasu rushes upon the left leg.
'Thou shalt sprinkle the left leg; then the Druj Nasu rushes upon the right ankle.
'Thou shalt sprinkle the right ankle; then the Druj Nasu rushes upon the left ankle.

24.
'Thou shalt sprinkle the left ankle; then the Druj Nasu rushes upon the right instep.
'Thou shalt sprinkle the right instep; then the Druj Nasu rushes upon the left instep.
'Thou shalt sprinkle the left instep; then the Druj Nasu turns round under the sole of the foot; it looks like the wing of a fly.

25.
'He shall press his toes upon the ground and shall raise up his heels; thou shalt sprinkle his right sole; then the Druj Nasu rushes upon the left sole.
'Thou shalt sprinkle the left sole; then the Druj Nasu turns round under the toes; it looks like the wing of a fly.

26.
'He shall press his heels upon the ground and shall raise

AVESTA: Vendidad

up his toes; thou shalt sprinkle his right toe; then the Druj
Nasu rushes upon the left toe.
'Thou shalt sprinkle the left toe; then the Druj Nasu flies away
to the regions of the north, in the shape of a raging fly, with
knees and tail sticking out, droning without end, and like unto
the foulest Khrafstras.
27.
'And thou shalt say these victorious, most healing words:
"'Yatha ahu vairyo: – The will of the Lord is the law of
righteousness.
"'The gifts of Vohu–mano to deeds done in this world for
Mazda.
"'He who relieves the poor makes Ahura king.
"'Kem–na mazda: – What protector hadst thou given unto me,
O Mazda! while the hate of the wicked encompasses me? Whom, but

thy Atar and Vohu–mano, through whose work I keep on the world
of Righteousness? Reveal therefore to me thy Religion as thy rule!

"'Ke verethrem–ja: – Who is the victorious who will protect
thy teaching? Make it clear that I am the guide for both worlds.
May Sraosha come with Vohu–mano and help whomsoever thou pleasest,
O Mazda!
"'Keep us from our hater, O Mazda and Armaiti Spenta! Perish,
O fiendish Druj! Perish, O brood of the fiend! Perish, O world
of the fiend! Perish away, O Druj! Rush away, O Druj! Perish away,
O Druj! Perish away to the regions of the north, never more to
give unto death the living world of Righteousness!"
28.
'At the first hole the man becomes freer from the Nasu; then
thou shalt say those victorious, most healing words: – "Yatha
ahu vairyo."
'At the second hole he becomes freer from the Nasu; then thou
shalt say those victorious, most healing words: – "Yatha
ahu vairyo,"
'At the third hole he becomes freer from the Nasu; then thou shalt

say those victorious, most healing words: –
"Yatha ahu vairyo,"
'At the fourth hole he becomes freer from the Nasu; then thou
shalt say those victorious, most healing words: –
"Yatha ahu vairyo,"
'At the fifth hole he becomes freer from the Nasu; then thou shalt
say those victorious, most healing words: –
"Yatha ahu vairyo,"
'At the sixth hole he becomes freer from the Nasu; then thou shalt
say those victorious, most healing words: – "Yatha ahu vairyo,"
 29.
'Afterwards the man defiled shall sit down, inside the furrows,
outside the furrows of the six holes, four fingers from those
furrows. There he shall cleanse his body with thick handfuls of
dust.
30.
'Fifteen times shall they take up dust from the ground for
him to rub his body, and they shall wait there until he is dry
even to the last hair on his head.
31.
'When his body is dry with dust, then he shall step over the
holes (containing water). At the first hole he shall wash his
body once with water; at the second hole he shall wash his body
twice with water; at the third hole he shall wash his body thrice
with water.
32.
'Then he shall perfume (his body) with Urvasna, or Vohu-gaona,
or Vohu-kereti, or Hadha-naepata, or any other sweet-smelling
plant; then he shall put on his clothes, and shall go back to
his house.
33.
'He shall sit down there in the place of infirmity, inside
the house, apart from the other worshippers of Mazda. He shall
not go near the fire, nor near the water, nor near the earth,
nor near the cow, nor near the trees, nor near the faithful, either
man or woman. Thus shall he continue until three nights have passed.

AVESTA: Vendidad

When three nights have passed, he shall wash his body, he shall wash his clothes with gomez and water to make them clean.

34.

'Then he shall sit down again in the place of infirmity, inside the house, apart from the other worshippers of Mazda. He shall not go near the fire, nor near the water, nor near the earth, nor near the cow, nor near the trees, nor near the faithful, either man or woman. Thus shall he continue until six nights have passed. When six nights have passed, he shall wash his body, he shall wash his clothes with gomez and water to make them clean.

35.

'Then he shall sit down again in the place of infirmity, inside the house, apart from the other worshippers of Mazda. He shall not go near the fire, nor near the water, nor near the earth, nor near the cow, nor near the trees, nor near the faithful, either man or woman. Thus shall he continue, until nine nights have passed. When nine nights have passed, he shall wash his body, he shall wash his clothes with gomez and water to make them clean.

36.

'He may thenceforth go near the fire, near the water, near the earth, near the cow, near the trees, and near the faithful, either man or woman.

II.

37.

'Thou shalt cleanse a priest for a blessing of the just.

'Thou shalt cleanse the lord of a province for the value of a camel of high value.

'Thou shalt cleanse the lord of a town for the value of a stallion of high value.

'Thou shalt cleanse the lord of a borough for the value of a bull of high value.

'Thou shalt cleanse the master of a house for the value of a cow three years old.

38.

AVESTA: Vendidad

'Thou shalt cleanse the wife of the master of a house for
the value of a ploughing cow.
'Thou shalt cleanse a menial for the value of a draught cow. 'Thou
shalt cleanse a young child for the value of a lamb.
39.
'These are the heads of cattle – flocks or herds – that the
worshippers of Mazda shall give to the man who has cleansed them,
if they can afford it; if they cannot afford it, they shall give
him any other value that may make him leave their houses well
pleased with them, and free from anger.
40.
'For if the man who has cleansed them leave their houses displeased
with them, and full of anger, then the Druj Nasu enters them from
the nose [of the dead], from the eyes, from the tongue, from the
jaws, from the sexual organs, from the hinder parts.
41.
'And the Druj Nasu rushes upon them even to the end of the
nails, and they are unclean thenceforth for ever and ever.
'It grieves the sun indeed, O Spitama Zarathushtra! to shine upon
a man defiled by the dead; it grieves the moon, it grieves the
stars.
42.
'That man delights them, O Spitama Zarathushtra! who cleanses
from the Nasu the man defiled by the dead; he delights the fire,
he delights the water, he delights the earth, he delights the
cow, he delights the trees, he delights the faithful, both men
and women.'
43.
Zarathushtra asked Ahura Mazda: 'O Maker of the material world,
thou Holy One! What shall be his reward, after his soul has parted
from his body, who has cleansed from the Nasu the man defiled
by the dead?'
44.
Ahura Mazda answered: 'The welfare of Paradise thou canst
promise to that man, for his reward in the other world.'
45.

AVESTA: Vendidad

Zarathushtra asked Ahura Mazda: 'O Maker of the material world, thou Holy One! How shall I fight against that Druj who from the dead rushes upon the living? How shall I fight against that Nasu who from the dead defiles the living?'

46.

Ahura Mazda answered: 'Say aloud those words in the Gathas that are to be said twice.

'Say aloud those words in the Gathas that are to be said thrice.

'Say aloud those words in the Gathas that are to be said four times.

'And the Druj shall fly away like the well-darted arrow, like the felt of last year, like the annual garment of the earth.'

III

47.

O Maker of the material world, thou Holy One! If a man who does not know the rites of cleansing according to the law of Mazda, offers to cleanse the unclean, how shall I then fight against that Druj who from the dead rushes upon the living? How shall I fight against that Druj who from the dead defiles the living?

48.

Ahura Mazda answered : 'Then, O Spitama Zarathushtra! the Druj Nasu appears to wax stronger than she was before. Stronger then are sickness and death and the working of the fiend than they were before.'

49.

O Maker of the material world, thou Holy One! What is the penalty that he shall pay?

Ahura Mazda answered: 'The worshippers of Mazda shall bind him; they shall bind his hands first; then they shall strip him of his clothes, they shall cut the head off his neck, and they shall give over his corpse unto the greediest of the corpse-eating creatures made by the beneficent Spirit, unto the vultures, with these words:
—

AVESTA: Vendidad

'"The man here has repented of all his evil thoughts, words, and deeds.

50.

'"If he has committed any other evil deed, it is remitted by his repentance; if he has committed no other evil deed, he is absolved by his repentance for ever and ever."'

51.

Who is he, O Ahura Mazda! who threatens to take away fullness and increase from the world, and to bring in sickness and death?

52.

Ahura Mazda answered: 'It is the ungodly Ashemaogha, O Spitama Zarathushtra! who in this material world cleanses the unclean without knowing the rites of cleansing according to the law of Mazda.

53.

'For until then, O Spitama Zarathushtra! sweetness and fatness would flow out from that land and from those fields, with health and healing, with fullness and increase and growth, and a growing of corn and grass.'

54.

O Maker of the material world, thou Holy One! When are sweetness and fatness to come back again to that land and to those fields, with health and healing, with fullness and increase and growth, and a growing of corn and grass?

55, 56.

Ahura Mazda answered: 'Sweetness and fatness will never come back again to that land and to those fields, with health and healing, with fullness and increase and growth, and a growing of corn and grass, until that ungodly Ashemaogha has been smitten to death on the spot, and the holy Sraosha of that place has been offered up a sacrifice, for three days and three nights, with fire blazing, with Baresma tied up, and with Haoma prepared. 57. 'Then sweetness and fatness will come back again to that land and to those fields, with health and healing, with fullness and increase and growth, and a growing of corn and grass.'

AVESTA: Vendidad

FARGARD 10. Formulas recited during the process of cleansing

1.
Zarathushtra asked Ahura Mazda: 'O Ahura Mazda! most beneficent Spirit, Maker of the material world, thou Holy One! How shall I fight against that Druj who from the dead rushes upon the living? How shall I fight against that Druj who from the dead defiles the living?'
2.
Ahura Mazda answered: 'Say aloud those words in the Gathas that are to be said twice.
'Say aloud those words in the Gathas that are to be said thrice'.

'Say aloud those words in the Gathas that are to be said four times.'
3.
O Maker of the material world, thou Holy One! Which are those words in the Gathas that are to be said twice? 4.

Ahura Mazda answered: 'These are the words in the Gathas that are to be said twice, and thou shalt twice say them aloud:–
ahya yasa ... urvanem (Y28.2).

---

humatenam ... mahi (Y35.2),
ashahya aad saire ... ahubya (Y35.8),
yatha tu i ... ahura (Y39.4),
humaim thwa ... hudaustema (Y41.3),
thwoi staotaraska ... ahura (Y41.5).

AVESTA: Vendidad

usta ahmai ... manangho (Y43.1),
spenta mainyu ... ahuro (Y47.1),
vohu khshathrem ... vareshane (Y51.1),
vahista istis ... skyaothanaka (Y53.1).

5.
'And after thou hast twice said those Bis-amrutas, thou shalt say aloud these victorious, most healing words:—
"'I drive away Angra Mainyu from this house, from this borough, from this town, from this land; from the very body of the man defiled by the dead, from the very body of the woman defiled by the dead; from the master of the house, from the lord of the borough, from the lord of the town, from the lord of the land; from the whole of the world of Righteousness.

6.
"'I drive away the Nasu, I drive away direct defilement, I drive away indirect defilement, from this house, from this borough, from this town, from this land; from the very body of the man defiled by the dead, from the very body of the woman defiled by the dead; from the master of the house, from the lord of the borough, from the lord of the town, from the lord of the land; from the whole of the world of Righteousness."'

7.
O Maker of the material world, thou Holy One! Which are those words in the Gathas that are to be said thrice?

8.
Ahura Mazda answered: 'These are the words in the Gathas that are to be said thrice, and thou shalt thrice say them aloud:—

ashem vohu ... (Y27.14),
ye sevisto ... paiti (Y33.11),
hukhshathrotemai ... vahistai (Y35.5),
duzvarenais ... vahyo (Y53.9).

9.

AVESTA: Vendidad

'After thou hast thrice said those Thris–amrutas, thou shalt
say aloud these victorious, most healing words:–
"'I drive away Indra, I drive away Sauru, I drive away the
Daeva Naunghaithya, from this house, from this borough, from this
town, from this land; from the very body of the man defiled by
the dead, from the very body of the woman defiled by the dead;
from the master of the house, from the lord of the borough, from
the lord of the town, from the lord of the land; from the whole
of the world of Righteousness.
10.
"'I drive away Tauru, I drive away Zairi, from this house,
from this borough, from this town, from this land; from the very
body of the man defiled by the dead, from the very body of the
woman defiled by the dead; from the master of the house, from
the lord of the borough, from the lord of the town, from the lord
of the land; from the whole of the holy world."'

11.
O Maker of the material world, thou Holy One! Which are those
words in the Gathas that are to be said four times?
12.
Ahura Mazda answered: 'These are the words in the Gathas that
are to be said four times, and thou shalt four times say them
aloud:–
yatha ahu vairyo ... (Y27.13),
mazda ad moi ... dau ahum (Y34.15),
a airyama ishyo ... masata mazdau (Y54.1).
13.
'After thou hast said those Chathrus–amratas four times, thou
shalt say aloud these victorious, most healing words:–
"'I drive away Aeshma, the fiend of the murderous spear,
I drive away the Daeva Akatasha, from this house, from this borough,
from this town, from this land; from the very body of the man
defiled by the dead, from the very body of the woman defiled by
the dead; from the master of the house, from the lord of the borough,

AVESTA: Vendidad

from the lord of the town, from the lord of the land; from the whole of the world of Righteousness.

14.

"'I drive away the Varenya Daevas, I drive away the wind–Daeva, from this house, from this borough, from this town, from this land; from the very body of the man defiled by the dead, from the very body of the woman defiled by the dead; from the master of the house, from the lord of the borough, from the lord of the town, from the lord of the land; from the whole of the world of Righteousness."

15.

'These are the words in the Gathas that are to be said twice; these are the words in the Gathas that are to be said thrice; these are the words in the Gathas that are to be said four times.

16.

'These are the words that smite down Angra Mainyu; these are the words that smite down Aeshma, the fiend of the murderous spear; these are the words that smite down the Daevas of Mazana; these are the words that smite down all the Daevas.

17.

'These are the words that stand, against that Druj, against that Nasu, who from the dead rushes upon the living, who from the dead defiles the living.

18.

'Therefore, O Zarathushtra! thou shalt dig nine holes in the part of the ground where there is least water and where there are fewest trees; where there is nothing that may be food either for man or beast; "for purity is for man, next to life, the, greatest good, that purity, O Zarathushtra, that is in the Religion of Mazda for him who cleanses his own self with good thoughts, words, and deeds."

19.

'Make thy own self pure, O righteous man! any one in the world here below can win purity for his own self, namely, when he cleanses his own self with good thoughts, words, and deeds.

20.

"'Yatha ahu vairyo: – The will of the Lord is the law
of righteousness,"
"'Kem–na Mazda: – What protector hast thou given unto me,
O Mazda! while the hate of the wicked encompasses me?"
"'Ke verethrem–ja: – Who is the victorious who will protect
thy teaching?"
"'Keep us from our hater, O Mazda and Armaiti Spenta! Perish,
O fiendish Druj! ... Perish away to the regions of the north,
never more to give unto death the living world of Righteousness!'"

FARGARD 11. Special formulas for cleansing several objects

1.
Zarathushtra asked Ahura Mazda: 'O Ahura Mazda! most beneficent
spirit, Maker of the material world, thou Holy One! How shall
I cleanse the house? how the fire? how the water? how the earth?
how the cow? how the tree? how the faithful man and the faithful
woman : how the stars? how the moon? how the sun? how the boundless
light? how all good things, made by Mazda, the offspring of the
holy principle?'
2.
Ahura Mazda answered: 'Thou shalt chant the cleansing words,
and the house shall be clean; clean shall be the fire, clean the
water, clean the earth, clean the cow, clean the tree, clean the
faithful man and the faithful woman, clean the stars, clean the
moon, clean the sun, clean the boundless light, clean all good
things, made by Mazda, the offspring of the holy principle.
3.
['So thou shalt say these victorious, most healing words];
thou shalt chant the Ahuna–Vairya five times: "The will of
the Lord is the law of righteousness,"

AVESTA: Vendidad

'The Ahuna–Vairya preserves the person of man:
'"Yatha ahu vairyo: – The will of the Lord is the law of righteousness,"
'"Kem–na Mazda: – What protector hast thou given unto me, O Mazda! while the hate of the wicked encompasses me?"
'"Ke verethrem–ja: – Who is the victorious who will protect thy teaching?"
'"Keep us from our hater, O Mazda and Armaiti Spenta!"

4.
'If thou wantest to cleanse the house, say these words aloud: "As long as the sickness lasts my great protector [is he who teaches virtue to the perverse]2."
'If thou wantest to cleanse the fire, say these words aloud: "Thy fire, first of all, do we approach with worship, O Ahura Mazda!"
5.
'If thou wantest to cleanse the water, say these words aloud: " Waters we worship, the Maekainti waters, the Hebvainti waters, the Fravazah waters."
'If thou wantest to cleanse the earth, say these words aloud: "This earth we worship, this earth with the women, this earth which bears us and those women who are thine, O Ahura!"
6.
'If thou wantest to cleanse the cow, say these words aloud: "The best of all works we will fulfill while we order both the learned and the unlearned, both masters and servants to secure for the cattle a good resting–place and fodder."
'If thou wantest to cleanse the trees, say these words aloud: "For him, as a reward, Mazda made the plants grow up."
7.
'If thou wantest to cleanse the faithful man or the faithful woman, say these words aloud: "May the vow–fulfilling Airyaman come hither, for the men and women of Zarathushtra to rejoice, for Vohu–mano to rejoice; with the desirable reward that Religion

AVESTA: Vendidad

deserves. I solicit for holiness that boon that is vouchsafed by Ahura!"

8.

'Then thou shalt say these victorious, most healing words. Thou shalt chant the Ahuna-Vairya eight times:—

"'Yatha ahu vairya:— The will of the Lord is the law of righteousness,"

"'Kem-na Mazda:— Whom hast thou placed to protect me, O Mazda?"

"'Ke verethrem-ja:— What protector hast thou given unto me?"

"'Who is the victorious?"
"'Keep us from our hater, O Mazda!" 9.
'I drive away Aeshma, I drive away the Nasu, I drive away direct defilement, I drive away indirect defilement.
['I drive away Khru, I drive away Khruighni.
'I drive away Buidhi, I drive away the offspring of Buidhi.
'I drive away Kundi, I drive away the offspring of Kundi.]
'I drive away the gaunt Bushyasta, I drive away the long-handed Bushyasta; [I drive away Muidhi, I drive away Kapasti.]
'I drive away the Pairika that comes upon the fire, upon the water, upon the earth, upon the cow, upon the tree. I drive away the uncleanness that comes upon the fire, upon the water, upon the earth, upon the cow, upon the tree.

10.

'I drive thee away, O mischievous Angra Mainyu! from the fire, from the water, from the earth, from the cow, from the tree, from the faithful man and from the faithful woman, from the stars, from the moon, from the sun, from the boundless light, from all good things, made by Mazda, the offspring of the holy principle.

11.

'Then thou shalt say these victorious, most healing words; thou shalt chant four Ahuna-Vairyas:—

"'Yatha aha vairyo:— The will of the Lord is the law of righteousness,"

"'Kem-na Mazda:— What protector hast thou given unto me?"

AVESTA: Vendidad

'"Ke verethrem–ja:– Who is the victorious?"
'"Keep us from our hater, O Mazda!" 12.
'Aeshma is driven away; away the Nasu; away direct defilement,
away indirect defilement.
['Khru is driven away, away Khruighni; away Buidhi, away the offspring
of Buidhi; away Kundi, away the offspring of Kundi.]
'The gaunt Bushyasta is driven away; away Bushyasta, the long–handed;
[away Muidhi, away Kapasti.]
'The Pairika is driven away that comes upon the fire, upon the
water, upon the earth, upon the cow, upon the tree. The uncleanness
is driven away that comes upon the fire, upon the water, upon
the earth, upon the cow, upon the tree.
13.
'Thou art driven away, O mischievous Angra Mainyu! from the
fire, from the water, from the earth, from the cow, from the tree,
from the faithful man and from the faithful woman, from the stars,
from the moon, from the sun, from the boundless light, from all
good things, made by Mazda, the offspring of the holy principle.
14.
'Then thou shalt say these victorious, most healing words;
thou shalt chant "Mazda ad moi" four times: "O
Mazda! say unto me the excellent words and the excellent works,
that through the good thought and the holiness of him who offers
thee the due meed of praise, thou mayest, O Lord! make the world
of Resurrection appear, at thy will, under thy sovereign rule."
15.
'I drive away Aeshma, I drive away the Nasu,' 16.
'I drive thee away, O mischievous Angra Mainyu! from the fire,
from the water,' 17.
'Then thou shalt say these victorious, most healing words;
thou shalt chant the Airyama Ishyo four times: "May the vow–fulfilling
Airyaman come hither!"' 18.
'Aeshma is driven away; away the Nasu,' 19.
'Thou art driven away, O mischievous Angra Mainyu! from the
fire, from the water,' 20.

AVESTA: Vendidad

'Then thou shalt say these victorious, most healing words;
thou shalt chant five Ahuna–Vairyas:–
"'Yatha ahu vairyo:– The will of the Lord is the law of righteousness,"

"'Kem–na Mazda:– Whom hast thou placed to protect me?"

"'Ke verethrem–ja:– Who is he who will smite the fiend?"

"'Keep us from our hater, O Mazda and Armaiti Spenta! Perish,
O fiendish Druj! Perish, O brood of the fiend! Perish, O world
of the fiend! Perish away, O Druj! Rush away, O Druj! Perish away,
O Druj! Perish away to the regions of the north, never more to
give unto death the living world of Righteousness!"'

FARGARD 12. The Upaman: how long it lasts for different relatives

1.
If one's father or mother dies, how long shall they stay [in
mourning], the son for his father, the daughter for her mother?
How long for the righteous? How long for the sinners?
Ahura Mazda answered: 'They shall stay thirty days for the righteous,
sixty days for the sinners.'
2.
O Maker of the material world, thou Holy One! How shall I
cleanse the house? How shall it be clean again?
Ahura Mazda answered: 'You shall wash your bodies three times,
you shall wash your clothes three times you shall chant the Gathas
three times; you shall offer up a sacrifice to my Fire, you shall
bind the bundles of Baresma, you shall bring libations to the
good waters; then the house shall be clean, and then the waters
may enter, then the fire may enter, and then the Amesha–Spentas

AVESTA: Vendidad

may enter, O Spitama Zarathushtra!'

3.

If one's son or daughter dies, how long shall they stay, the father for his son, the mother for her daughter? How long for the righteous? How long for the sinners?

Ahura Mazda answered: 'They shall stay thirty days for the righteous, sixty days for the sinners.'

4.

O Maker of the material world, thou Holy One! How shall I cleanse the house? How shall it be clean again?

Ahura Mazda answered: 'You shall wash your bodies three times, you shall wash your clothes three times, you shall chant the Gathas three times; you shall offer up a sacrifice to my Fire, you shall bind up the bundles of Baresma, you shall bring libations to the good waters; then the house shall be clean, and then the waters may enter, then the fire may enter, and then the Amesha–Spentas may enter, O Spitama Zarathushtra!'

5.

If one's brother or sister dies, how long shall they stay, the brother for his brother, the sister for her sister? How long for the righteous? How long for the sinners?

Ahura Mazda answered: 'They shall stay thirty days for the righteous, sixty days for the sinners.'

6.

O Maker of the material world, thou Holy One! How shall I cleanse the house? How shall it be clean again? Ahura Mazda answered: 'You shall wash your bodies three times, you shall wash your clothes three times, you shall chant the Gathas three times; you shall offer up a sacrifice to my Fire, you shall bind up the bundles of Baresma, you shall bring libations to the good waters; then the house shall be clean, and then the waters may enter, then the fire may enter, and then the Amesha–Spentas may enter, O Spitama Zarathushtra!'

7.

If the master of the house dies, or if the mistress of the house dies, how long shall they stay? How long for the righteous?

AVESTA: Vendidad

How long for the sinners?
Ahura Mazda answered: 'They shall stay six months for the righteous, a year for the sinners.'
8.
O Maker of the material world, thou Holy One! How shall I cleanse the house? How shall it be clean again?
Ahura Mazda answered: 'you shall wash your bodies three times, you shall wash your clothes three times, you shall chant the Gathas three times; you shall offer up a sacrifice to my Fire, you shall bind up the bundles of Baresma, you shall bring libations to the good waters; then the house shall be clean, and then the waters may enter, then the fire may enter, and then the Amesha−Spentas may enter, O Spitama Zarathushtra!'
9.
If one's grandfather or grandmother dies, how long shall they stay, the grandson for his grandfather, the granddaughter for her grandmother? How long for the righteous? How long for the sinners?
Ahura Mazda answered: 'They shall stay twenty−five days for the righteous, fifty days for the sinners.'
10.
O Maker of the material world, thou Holy One! How shall I cleanse the house? How shall it be clean again?
Ahura Mazda answered: 'You shall wash your bodies three times, you shall wash your clothes three times, you shall chant the Gathas three times; you shall offer up a sacrifice to my Fire, you shall bind up the bundles of Baresma, you shall bring libations to the good waters; then the house shall be clean, and then the waters may enter, then the fire may enter, and then the Amesha−Spentas may enter, O Spitama Zarathushtra!'
11.
If one's grandson or granddaughter dies, how long shall they stay, the grandfather for his grandson, the grandmother for her granddaughter? How long for the righteous? How long for the sinners?

Ahura Mazda answered: 'They shall stay twenty−five days for the

AVESTA: Vendidad

righteous, fifty days for the sinners.'

12.
O Maker of the material world, thou Holy One! How shall I cleanse the house? How shall it be clean again?
Ahura Mazda answered: 'You shall wash your bodies three times, you shall wash your clothes three times, you shall chant the Gathas three times; you shall offer up a sacrifice to my Fire, you shall bind up the bundles of Baresma, you shall bring libations to the good waters; then the house shall be clean, and then the waters may enter, then the fire may enter, and then the Amesha-Spentas may enter, O Spitama Zarathushtra!'

13.
If one's uncle or aunt dies, how long shall they stay, the nephew for his uncle, the niece for her aunt? How long for the righteous? How long for the sinners?
Ahura Mazda answered: 'They shall stay twenty days for the righteous, forty days for the sinners.'

14.
O Maker of the material world, thou Holy One! How shall I cleanse the house? How shall it be clean again?
Ahura Mazda answered: 'You shall wash your bodies three times, you shall wash your clothes three times, you shall chant the Gathas three times; you shall offer up a sacrifice to my Fire, you shall bind up the bundles of Baresma, you shall bring libations to the good waters; then the house shall be clean, and then the waters may enter, then the fire may enter, and then the Amesha-Spentas may enter, O Spitama Zarathushtra!'

15.
If one's male cousin or female cousin dies, how long shall they stay? How long for the righteous? How long for the sinners?

Ahura Mazda answered: 'They shall stay fifteen days for the righteous, thirty days for the sinners.'

16.
O Maker of the material world, thou Holy One! How shall I cleanse the house? How shall it be clean again?

AVESTA: Vendidad

Ahura Mazda answered: 'You shall wash your bodies three times, you shall wash your clothes three times, you shall chant the Gathas three times; you shall offer up a sacrifice to my Fire, you shall bind up the bundles of Baresma, you shall bring libations to the good waters; then the house shall be clean, and then the waters may enter, then the fire may enter, and then the Amesha–Spentas may enter, O Spitama Zarathushtra!'
17.
If the son or the daughter of a cousin dies, how long shall they stay? How long for the righteous: How long for the sinners?

Ahura Mazda answered: 'They shall stay ten days for the righteous, twenty days for the sinners.'
18.
O Maker of the material world, thou Holy One! How shall I cleanse the house? How shall it be clean again?
Ahura Mazda answered: 'You shall wash your bodies three times, you shall wash your clothes three times, you shall chant the Gathas three times; you shall offer up a sacrifice to my Fire, you shall bind up the bundles of Baresma, you shall bring libations to the good waters; then the house shall be clean, and then the waters may enter, then the fire may enter, and then the Amesha–Spentas may enter, O Spitama Zarathushtra!'
19.
If the grandson of a cousin or the granddaughter of a cousin dies, how long shall they stay? How long for the righteous? How long for the sinners?
Ahura Mazda answered: 'They shall stay five days for the righteous, ten days for the sinners.'
20.
O Maker of the material world, thou Holy One! How shall I cleanse the house? How shall it be clean again?
Ahura Mazda answered: 'You shall wash your bodies three times, you shall wash your clothes three times, you shall chant the Gathas three times; you shall offer up a sacrifice to my Fire, you shall bind up the bundles of Baresma, you shall bring libations to the

good waters; then the house shall be clean, and then the waters may enter, then the fire may enter, and then the Amesha-Spentas may enter, O Spitama Zarathushtra!'

21.

If a man dies, of whatever race he is, who does not belong to the true faith, or the true law, what part of the creation of the good spirit does he directly defile? What part does he indirectly defile?

22.

Ahura Mazda answered: 'No more than a frog does whose venom is dried up, and that has been dead more than a year. Whilst alive, indeed, O Spitama Zarathushtra! such wicked, two-legged ruffian as an ungodly Ashemaogha, directly defiles the creatures of the Good Spirit, and indirectly defiles them.

23.

'Whilst alive he smites the water; whilst alive he blows out the fire; whilst alive he carries off the cow; whilst alive he smites the faithful man with a deadly blow, that parts the soul from the body; not so will he do when dead.

24.

'Whilst alive, indeed, O Spitama Zarathushtra! such wicked, two-legged ruffian as an ungodly Ashemaogha, robs the faithful man of the full possession of his food, of his clothing, of his wood, of his bed, of his vessels; not so will he do when dead.'

FARGARD 13. The Dog.

Ia.

1.

Which is the good creature among the creatures of the Good Spirit that from midnight till the sun is up goes and kills thousands of the creatures of the Evil Spirit?

AVESTA: Vendidad

2.
Ahura Mazda answered: 'The dog with the prickly back, with the long and thin muzzle, the dog Vanghapara, which evil-speaking people call the Duzaka; this is the good creature among the creatures of the Good Spirit that from midnight till the sun is up goes and kills thousands of the creatures of the Evil Spirit.

3.
'And whosoever, O Zarathushtra! shall kill the dog with the prickly back, with the long and thin muzzle, the dog Vanghapara, which evil-speaking people call the Duzaka, kills his own soul for nine generations, nor shall he find a way over the Chinwad bridge, unless he has, while alive, atoned for his sin.'

4.
O Maker of the material world, thou Holy One! If a man kill the dog with the prickly back, with the long and thin muzzle, the dog Vanghapara, which evil-speaking people call the Duzaka, what is the penalty that he shall pay?
Ahura Mazda answered: 'A thousand stripes with the Aspahe-astra, a thousand stripes with the Sraosho-charana.

Ib.

5.
Which is the evil creature among the creatures of the Evil Spirit that from midnight till the sun is up goes and kills thousands of the creatures of the Good Spirit?

6.
Ahura Mazda answered: 'The Daeva Zairimyangura, which evil-speaking people call the Zairimyaka, this is the evil creature among the creatures of the Evil Spirit that from midnight till the sun is up goes and kills thousands of the creatures of the Good Spirit.

7.
'And whosoever, O Zarathushtra! shall kill the Daeva Zairimyangura, which evil-speaking people call the Zairimyaka, his sins in thought, word, and deed are redeemed as they would be by a Patet; his sins in thought, word, and deed are atoned for.

AVESTA: Vendidad

II.

8.
'Whosoever shall smite either a shepherd's dog, or a house–dog, or a Vohunazga dog, or a trained dog, his soul when passing to the other world, shall fly howling louder and more sorely grieved than the sheep does in the lofty forest where the wolf ranges.

9.
'No soul will come and meet his departing soul and help it, howling and grieved in the other world; nor will the dogs that keep the [Chinwad] bridge help his departing soul howling and grieved in the other world.

10.
'If a man shall smite a shepherd's dog so that it becomes unfit for work, if he shall cut off its ear or its paw, and thereupon a thief or a wolf break in and carry away [sheep] from the fold, without the dog giving any warning, the man shall pay for the loss, and he shall pay for the wound of the dog as for willful wounding.

11.
'If a man shall smite a house–dog so that it becomes unfit for work, if he shall cut off its ear or its paw, and thereupon a thief or a wolf break in and carry away [anything] from the house, without the dog giving any warning, the man shall pay for the loss, and he shall pay for the wound of the dog as for willful wounding.'

12.
O Maker of the material world, thou Holy One! If a man shall smite a shepherd's dog, so that it gives up the ghost and the soul parts from the body, what is the penalty that he shall pay?

Ahura Mazda answered: 'Eight hundred stripes with the Aspahe–astra, eight hundred stripes with the Sraosho–charana.'

13.
O Maker of the material world, thou Holy One! If a man shall

AVESTA: Vendidad

smite a house–dog so that it gives up the ghost and the soul parts from the body, what is the penalty that he shall pay?
Ahura Mazda answered; 'Seven hundred stripes with the Aspahe–astra, seven hundred stripes with the Sraosho–charana.'
14.
O Maker of the material world, thou Holy One! If a man shall smite a Vohunazga dog so that it gives up the ghost and the soul parts from the body, what is the penalty that he shall pay?
Ahura Mazda answered: 'Six hundred stripes with the Aspahe–astra, six hundred stripes with the Sraosho–charana.'
15.
O Maker of the material world, thou Holy One! If a man shall smite a Tauruna dog so that it gives up the ghost and the soul parts from the body, what is the penalty that he shall pay?
Ahura Mazda answered: 'Five hundred stripes with the Aspahe–astra, five hundred stripes with the Sraosho–charana.'
16.
'This is the penalty for the murder of a Gazu dog, of a Vizu dog, of a porcupine dog, of a sharptoothed weasel, of a swift–running fox; this is the penalty for the murder of any of the creatures of the Good Spirit belonging to the dog kind, except the water–dog.'

III.
17.
O Maker of the material world, thou Holy One! What is the place of the shepherd's dog?
Ahura Mazda answered: 'He comes and goes a Yugyesti round about the fold, watching for the thief and the wolf.'
18.
O Maker of the material world, thou Holy One! What is the place of the house–dog?
Ahura Mazda answered: 'He comes and goes a Hathra round about the house, watching for the thief and the wolf.'
19.
O Maker of the material world, thou Holy One! What is the

AVESTA: Vendidad

place of the Vohunazga dog?.
Ahura Mazda answered: 'He claims none of those talents, and only seeks for his subsistence.'

IV.
20.
O Maker of the material world, thou Holy One! If a man give bad food to a shepherd's dog, of what sin does he make himself guilty?
Ahura Mazda answered: 'He makes himself guilty of the same guilt as though he should serve bad food to a master of a house of the first rank.'
21.
O Maker of the material world, thou Holy One! If a man give bad food to a house–dog, of what sin does he make himself guilty?

Ahura Mazda answered: 'He makes himself guilty of the same guilt as though he should serve bad food to a master of a house of middle rank.'
22.
O Maker of the material world, thou Holy One! If a man give bad food to a Vohunazga dog, of what sin does he make himself guilty?
Ahura Mazda answered: 'He makes himself guilty of the same guilt as though he should serve bad food to a holy man, who should come to his house in the character of a priest.'
23.
O Maker of the material world, thou Holy One! If a man give bad food to a Tauruna dog, of what sin does he make himself guilty?

Ahura Mazda answered: 'He makes himself guilty of the same guilt as though he should serve bad food to a young man, born of pious parents, and who can already answer for his deeds.'
24.
O Maker of the material world, thou Holy One! If a man shall

AVESTA: Vendidad

give bad food to a shepherd's dog, what is the penalty that he shall pay?

Ahura Mazda answered: 'He is a Peshotanu: two hundred stripes with the Aspahe–astra, two hundred stripes with the Sraosho–charana.'

25.

O Maker of the material world, thou Holy One! If a man shall give bad food to a house–dog, what is the penalty that he shall pay?

Ahura Mazda answered: 'Ninety stripes with the Aspahe–astra, ninety stripes with the Sraosho–charana.'

26.

O Maker of the material world, thou Holy One! If a man shall give bad food to a Vohunazga dog, what is the penalty that he shall pay?

Ahura Mazda answered: 'Seventy stripes with the Aspahe–astra, seventy stripes with the Sraosho–charana.'

27.

O Maker of the material world, thou Holy One! If a man shall give bad food to a Tauruna dog, what is the penalty that he shall pay?

Ahura Mazda answered: 'Fifty stripes with the Aspahe–astra, fifty stripes with the Sraosho–charana.

28.

'For in this material world, O Spitama Zarathushtra! it is the dog, of all the–creatures of the Good Spirit, that most quickly decays into age, while not eating near eating people, and watching goods none of which it receives. Bring ye unto him milk and fat with meat; this is the right food for the dog.'

V.

29.

O Maker of the material world, thou Holy One! If there be in the house of a worshipper of Mazda a mad dog that bites without barking, what shall the worshippers of Mazda do?

30.

AVESTA: Vendidad

Ahura Mazda answered: 'They shall put a wooden collar around his neck, and they shall tie thereto a muzzle, an asti thick if the wood be hard, two astis thick if it be soft. To that collar they shall tie it; by the two sides of the collar they shall tie it.

31.
'If they shall not do so, and the mad dog that bites without barking, smite a sheep or wound a man, the dog shall pay for the wound of the wounded as for willful murder.

32.
'If the dog shall smite a sheep or wound a man, they shall cut off his right ear.
'If he shall smite another sheep or wound another man, they shall cut off his left ear.

33.
'If he shall smite a third sheep or wound a third man, they shall make a cut in his right foot. If he shall smite a fourth sheep or wound a fourth man, they shall make a cut in his left foot.

34.
'If he shall for the fifth time smite a sheep or wound a man, they shall cut off his tail.
'Therefore they shall tie a muzzle to the collar; by the two sides of the collar they shall tie it. If they shall not do so, and the mad dog that bites without barking, smite a sheep or wound a man, he shall pay for the wound of the wounded as for willful murder.'

35.
O Maker of the material world, thou Holy One! If there be in the house of a worshipper of Mazda a mad dog, who has no scent, what shall the worshippers of Mazda do?
Ahura Mazda answered: 'They shall attend him to heal him, in the same manner as they would do for one of the faithful.'

36.
O Maker of the material world, thou Holy One! If they try to heal him and fail, what shall the worshippers of Mazda do?

AVESTA: Vendidad

37.
Ahura Mazda answered: 'They shall put a wooden collar around his neck, and they shall tie thereto a muzzle, an asti thick if the wood be hard, two astis thick if it be soft. To that collar they shall tie it; by the two sides of the collar they shall tie it.

38.
'If they shall not do so, the scentless dog may fall into a hole, or a well, or a precipice, or a river, or a canal, and come to grief: if he come to grief so, they shall be therefore Peshotanus.

VI.

39.
'The dog, O Spitama Zarathushtra! I, Ahura Mazda, have made self-clothed and self-shod; watchful and wakeful; and sharp-toothed; born to take his food from man and to watch over man's goods. I, Ahura Mazda, have made the dog strong of body against the evil-doer, when sound of mind and watchful over your goods.

40.
'And whosoever shall awake at his voice, O Spitama Zarathushtra! neither shall the thief nor the wolf carry anything from his house, without his being warned; the wolf shall be smitten and torn to pieces; he is driven away, he melts away like snow.'

VII.

41.
O Maker of the material world, thou Holy One! Which of the two wolves deserves more to be killed, the one that a he-dog begets of a she-wolf, or the one that a he-wolf begets of a she-dog?

Ahura Mazda answered: 'Of these two wolves, the one that a he-dog begets of a she-wolf deserves more to be killed than the one that a he-wolf begets of a she-dog.

AVESTA: Vendidad

42.
'For the dogs born therefrom fall on the shepherd's dog, on the house–dog, on the Vohu–nazga dog, on the trained dog, and destroy the folds; such dogs are more murderous, more mischievous, more destructive to the folds than any other dogs.

43.
'And the wolves born therefrom fall on the shepherd's dog, on the house–dog, on the Vohunazga dog, on the trained dog, and destroy the folds; such wolves are more murderous, more mischievous, more destructive to the folds than any other wolves.

VIII.

44.
'A dog has the characters of eight sorts of people:–
'He has the character of a priest,
'He has the character of a warrior,
'He has the character of a husbandman,
'He has the character of a strolling singer,
'He has the character of a thief,
'He has the character of a disu,
'He has the character of a courtesan,
'He has the character of a child.

45.
'He eats the refuse, like a priest; he is easily satisfied, like a priest; he is patient, like a priest; he wants only a small piece of bread, like a priest; in these things he is like unto a priest.
'He marches in front, like a warrior; he fights for the beneficent cow, like a warrior; he goes first out of the house, like a warrior; in these things he is like unto a warrior.

46.
'He is watchful and sleeps lightly, like a husbandman; he goes first out of the house, like a husbandman; he returns last into the house, like a husbandman; in these things he is like unto a husbandman.

AVESTA: Vendidad

'He is fond of singing, like a strolling singer; he wounds him who gets too near, like a strolling singer; he is ill-trained, like a strolling singer; he is changeful, like a strolling singer; in these things he is like unto a strolling singer.

47.
'He is fond of darkness, like a thief; he prowls about in darkness, like a thief; he is a shameless eater, like a thief; he is therefore an unfaithful keeper, like a thief; in these things he is like unto a thief.

'He is fond of darkness, like a disu; he prowls about in darkness, like a disu; he is a shameless eater, like a disu; he is therefore an unfaithful keeper, like a disu; in these things he is like unto a disu.

48.
'He is fond of singing, like a courtesan; he wounds him who gets too near, like a courtesan; he roams along the roads, like a courtesan; he is ill-trained, like a courtesan; he is changeful, like a courtesan; in these things he is like unto a courtesan.

'He is fond of sleep, like a child; he is tender like snow, like a child; he is full of tongue, like a child; he digs the earth with his paws, like a child; in these things he is like unto a child.

IX.
49.
'If those two dogs of mine, the shepherd's dog and the house-dog, pass by any of my houses, let them never be kept away from it.

'For no house could subsist on the earth made by Ahura, but for those two dogs of mine, the shepherd's dog and the house-dog.'

X.
50.

AVESTA: Vendidad

O Maker of the material world, thou Holy One! When a dog dies,
with marrow and seed dried up, whereto does his ghost go?
51.
Ahura Mazda answered: 'It passes to the spring of the waters,
O Spitama Zarathushtra! and there out of them two water-dogs are
formed: out of every thousand dogs and every thousand she-dogs,
a couple is formed, a water-dog and a water she-dog.
52.
'He who kills a water-dog brings about a drought that dries
up pastures.
'Until then, O Spitama Zarathushtra! sweetness and fatness would
flow out from that land and from those fields, with health and
healing, with fullness and increase and growth, and a growing
of corn and grass.'
53.
O Maker of the material world, thou Holy One! When are sweetness
and fatness to come back again to that land and to those fields,
with health and healing, with fullness and increase and growth,
and a growing of corn and grass?
54, 55.
Ahura Mazda answered: 'Sweetness and fatness will never come
back again to that land and to those fields, with health and healing,
with fullness and increase and growth, and a growing of corn and
grass, until the murderer of the water-dog has been smitten to
death on the spot, and the holy soul of the dog has been offered
up a sacrifice, for three days and three nights, with fire blazing,
with Baresma tied up, and with Haoma prepared.
56.
['Then sweetness and fatness will come back again to that
land and to those fields, with health and healing, with fullness
and increase and growth, and a growing of corn and grass.']

AVESTA: Vendidad

FARGARD 14. Atoning for the murder of a water-dog

1.
Zarathushtra asked Ahura Mazda: 'O Ahura Mazda, most beneficent Spirit, Maker of the material world, thou Holy One! He who smites one of those water-dogs that are born one from a thousand dogs and a thousand she-dogs, so that he gives up the ghost and the soul parts from the body, what is the penalty that he shall pay?'
2.
Ahura Mazda answered: 'He shall pay ten thousand stripes with the Aspahe-astra, ten thousand stripes with the Sraosho-charana.

'He shall godly and piously bring unto the fire of Ahura Mazda ten thousand loads of hard, well dried, well examined wood, to redeem his own soul.
3.
'He shall godly and piously, bring unto the fire of Ahura Mazda ten thousand loads of soft wood, of Urvasna, Vohu-gaona, Vohu-kereti, Hadha-naepata, or any sweet-scented plant, to redeem his own soul.
4.
'He shall godly and piously tie ten thousand bundles of Baresma, to redeem his own soul.
'He shall offer up to the Good Waters ten thousand Zaothra libations with the Haoma and the milk, cleanly prepared and well strained, cleanly prepared and well strained by a pious man, and mixed with the roots of the tree known as Hadha-naepata, to redeem his own soul.
5.
'He shall kill ten thousand snakes of those that go upon the belly. He shall kill ten thousand Kahrpus, who are snakes with the shape of a dog. He shall hill ten thousand tortoises. He shall kill ten thousand land-frogs; he shall kill ten thousand water-frogs. He shall kill ten thousand corn-carrying ants; he shall kill ten

AVESTA: Vendidad

thousand ants of the small, venomous mischievous kind.
6.
'He shall kill ten thousand worms of those that live on dirt;
he shall kill ten thousand raging flies.
'He shall fill up ten thousand holes for the unclean.
'He shall godly and piously give to godly men twice the set of
seven implements for the fire, to redeem his own soul, namely:–
7.
'The two answering implements for fire; a broom; a pair of
tongs; a pair of round bellows extended at the bottom, contracted
at the top; a sharp-edged sharp-pointed adze; a sharp-toothed
sharp-pointed saw; by means of which the worshippers of Mazda
procure wood for the fire of Ahura Mazda.
8.
'He shall godly and piously give to godly men a set of the
priestly instruments of which the priests make use, to redeem
his own soul, namely: The Astra; the meat-vessel; the Paitidana;
the Khrafstraghna; the Sraosho-charana; the cup for the Myazda;
the cups for mixing and dividing; the regular mortar; the Haoma
cups; and the Baresma.
9.
'He shall godly and piously give to godly men a set of all
the war implements of which the warriors make use, to redeem his
own soul;
'The first being a javelin, the second a sword, the third a club,
the fourth a bow, the fifth a saddle with a quiver and thirty
brass-headed arrows, the sixth a sling with arm-string and with
thirty sling stones;
'The seventh a cuirass, the eighth a hauberk, the ninth a tunic,
the tenth a helmet, the eleventh a girdle, the twelfth a pair
of greaves.
10.
'He shall godly and piously give to godly men a set of all
the implements of which the husbandmen make use, to redeem his
own soul, namely: A plough with yoke and ...1; a goad for ox;
a mortar of stone; a round-headed hand-mill for grinding corn;

AVESTA: Vendidad

11.
'A spade for digging and tilling; one measure of silver and
one measure of gold.'
O Maker of the material world, thou Holy One! How much silver?

Ahura Mazda answered: 'The price of a stallion.'
O Maker of the material world, thou Holy One! How much gold?
Ahura Mazda answered: 'The price of a he-camel.
12.
'He shall godly and piously procure a rill of running water
for godly husbandmen, to redeem his own soul.'
O Maker of the material world, thou Holy One! How large is the
rill?
Ahura Mazda answered: 'The depth of a dog, and the breadth of
a dog.
13.
'He shall godly and piously give a piece of arable land to
godly men, to redeem his own soul.'
O Maker of the material world, thou Holy One! How large is the
piece of land?
Ahura Mazda answered: 'As much as can be watered with such a rill
divided into two canals.
14.
'He shall godly and piously procure for godly men a stable
for oxen, with nine hathras and nine nematas, to redeem his own
soul.'
O Maker of the material world, thou Holy One! How large is the
stable?
Ahura Mazda answered: 'It shall have twelve alleys in the largest
part of the house, nine alleys in the middle part, six alleys
in the smallest part.
'He shall godly and piously give to godly men goodly beds with
Sheets and cushions, to redeem his own soul.
15.
'He shall godly and piously give in marriage to a godly man
a virgin maid, whom no man has known, to redeem his own soul.'

O Maker of the material world, thou Holy One! What sort of maid?

Ahura Mazda answered: 'A sister or a daughter of his, at the age of puberty, with ear-rings in her ears and past her fifteenth year.
16.
'He shall godly and piously give to holy men twice seven head of small cattle, to redeem his own soul.'
'He shall bring up twice seven whelps.
'He shall throw twice seven bridges over canal.
17.
'He shall put into repair twice nine stables that are out of repair.
'He shall cleanse twice nine dogs from stipti, anairiti, and vyangura, and all the diseases that are produced on the body of a dog.
'He shall treat twice nine godly men to their fill of meat, bread, strong drink, and wine.
18.
'This is the penalty, this is the atonement which saves the faithful man who submits to it not him who does not submit to it. Such a one shall surely be an inhabitant in the mansion of the Druj.'

FARGARD 15. Regarding certain sins and obligations

I.
1.
How many are the sins that men commit and that, being committed and not confessed, nor atoned for, make their committer a Peshotanu?
2.
Ahura Mazda answered: 'There are five such sins, O holy Zarathushtra!

AVESTA: Vendidad

It is the first of these sins that men commit when a man teaches one of the faithful another faith, another law, a lower doctrine, and he leads him astray with a full knowledge and conscience of the sin: the man who has done the deed becomes a Peshotanu.
3.
'It is the second of these sins when a man gives bones too hard or food too hot to a shepherd's dog or to a house–dog;
4.
'If the bones stick in the dog's teeth or stop in his throat; or if the food too hot burn his mouth or his tongue, he may come to grief thereby; if he come to grief thereby, the man who has done the deed becomes a Peshotanu.
5.
'It is the third of these sins when a man smites a bitch big with young or affrights her by running after her, or shouting or clapping with the hands;
6.
'If the bitch fall into a hole, or a well, or a precipice, or a river, or a canal, she may come to grief thereby; if she come to grief thereby, the man who has done the deed becomes a Peshotanu.
7.
'It is the fourth of these sins when a man has intercourse with a woman who has the whites or sees the blood, the man that has done the deed becomes a Peshotanu.
8.
'It is the fifth of these sins when a man has intercourse with a woman quick with child, whether the milk has already come to her breasts or has not yet come: she may come to grief thereby; if she come to grief thereby, the man who has done the deed becomes a Peshotanu.

IIa.
9.
'If a man come near unto a damsel, either dependent on the

AVESTA: Vendidad

chief of the family or not dependent, either delivered [unto a husband] or not delivered, and she conceives by him, let her not, being ashamed of the people, produce in herself the menses, against the course of nature, by means of water and plants.

10.
'And if the damsel, being ashamed of the people, shall produce in herself the menses gainst the course of nature, by means of water and plants, it is a fresh sin as heavy [as the first]3.

11.
'If a man come near unto a damsel, either dependent on the chief of the family or not dependent, either delivered [unto a husband] or not delivered, and she conceives by him, let her not, being ashamed of the people, destroy the fruit in her womb.

12.
'And if the damsel, being ashamed of the people, shall destroy the fruit in her womb, the sin is on both the father and herself, the murder is on both the father and herself; both the father and herself shall pay the penalty for willful murder.

IIb.
13.
'If a man come near unto a damsel, either dependent on the chief of the family or not dependent, either delivered [unto a husband] or not delivered, and she conceives by him, and she says, "I have conceived by thee;" and he replies, "Go then to the old woman and apply to her for one of her drugs, that she may procure thee miscarriage;"

14.
'And the damsel goes to the old woman and applies to her for one of her drugs, that she may procure her miscarriage; and the old woman brings her some Banga, or Shaeta, a drug that kills in the womb or one that expels out of the womb, or some other of the drugs that produce miscarriage and [the man says], "Cause thy fruit to perish!" and she causes her fruit to perish; the sin is on the head of all three, the man, the damsel, and

AVESTA: Vendidad

the old woman.

15.

'If a man come near unto a damsel, either dependent on the chief of the family or not dependent, either delivered [unto a husband] or not delivered, and she conceives by him, so long shall he support her, until the child be born.

16.

'If he shall not support her, so that the child comes to grief, for want of proper support, he shall pay for it the penalty for willful murder.'

17.

O Maker of the material world, thou Holy One! If she be near her time, which is the worshipper of Mazda that shall support her?

18.

Ahura Mazda answered: 'If a man come near unto a damsel, either dependent on the chief of the family or not dependent, either delivered [unto a husband] or not delivered, and she conceives by him, so long shall he support her, until the child be born.

19.

'If he shall not support her ....

'It lies with the faithful to look in the same way after every pregnant female, either two–footed or four–footed, two–footed woman or four–footed bitch.'

III.

20.

O Maker of the material world, thou Holy One! If (a bitch) be near her time, which is the worshipper of Mazda that shall support her?

21.

Ahura Mazda answered: 'He whose house stands nearest, the care of supporting her is his; so long shall he support her, until the whelps be born.

22.

AVESTA: Vendidad

'If he shall not support her, so that the whelps come to grief, for want of proper support; he shall pay for it the penalty for willful murder.'

23.

O Maker of the material world, thou Holy One! If a bitch be near her time and be lying in a stable for camels, which is the worshipper of Mazda that shall support her?

24.

Ahura Mazda answered: 'He who built the stable for camels or whoso holds it, the care of supporting her is his; so long shall he support her, until the whelps be born.

25.

'If he shall not support her, so that the whelps come to grief, for want of proper support, he shall pay for it the penalty for willful murder.'

26.

O Maker of the material world, thou Holy One! If a bitch be near her time and be lying in a stable for horses, which is the worshipper of Mazda that shall support her?

27.

Ahura Mazda answered: 'He who built the stable for horses or whoso holds it, the care of supporting her is his; so long shall he support her, until the whelps be born.

28.

'If he shall not support her, so that the whelps come to grief, for want of proper support, he shall pay for it the penalty for willful murder.'

29.

O Maker of the material world, thou Holy One! If a bitch be near her time and be lying in a stable for oxen, which is the worshipper of Mazda that shall support her?

30.

Ahura Mazda answered: 'He who built the stable for oxen or whoso holds it, the care of supporting her is his; so long shall he support her, until the whelps be born.

31.

AVESTA: Vendidad

'If he shall not support her, so that the whelps come to grief, for want of proper support, he shall pay for it the penalty for willful murder.'

32.

O Maker of the material world, thou Holy One! If a bitch be near her time and be lying in a sheep-fold, which is the worshipper of Mazda that shall support her?

33.

Ahura Mazda answered: 'He who built the sheepfold or whoso holds it, the care of supporting her is his; so long shall he support her, until the whelps be born.

34.

'If he shall not support her so that the whelps come to grief, for want of proper support, he shall pay for it the penalty for willful murder.'

35.

O Maker of the material world, thou Holy One! If a bitch be near her time and be lying on the earth-wall, which is the worshipper of Mazda that shall support her?

36.

Ahura Mazda answered: 'He who erected the wall or whoso holds it, the care of supporting her is his; so long shall he support her, until the whelps be born.

37.

'If he shall not support her, so that the whelps come to grief, for want of proper support, he shall pay for it the penalty for willful murder.'

38.

O Maker of the material world, thou Holy One! If a bitch be near her time and be lying in the moat, which is the worshipper of Mazda that shall support her?

39.

Ahura Mazda answered: 'He who dug the moat or whoso holds it, the care of supporting her is his; so long shall he support her, until the whelps be born.

40.

'If he shall not support her, so that the whelps come to grief, for want of proper support, he shall pay for it the penalty for willful murder.'

41.
O Maker of the material world, thou Holy One! If a bitch be near her time and be lying in the middle of a pasture–field, which is the worshipper of Mazda that shall support her?

42.
Ahura Mazda answered: 'He who sowed the pasture–field or whoso holds it, the care of supporting her is his; [so long shall he support her, until the whelps be born. If he shall not support her, so that the whelps come to grief, for want of proper support, he shall pay for it the penalty for willful murder.]

43.
'He shall take her to rest upon a litter of nemovanta or of any foliage fit for a litter; so long shall he support her, until the young dogs are capable of self–defense and self–subsistence.'

44.
O Maker of the material world, thou Holy One! When are the dogs capable of self–defense and self–subsistence?

45.
Ahura Mazda answered: 'When they are able to run about in a circuit of twice seven houses around. Then they may be let loose, whether it be winter or summer.

'Young dogs ought to be supported for six months, children for seven years.

'Atar, the son of Ahura Mazda, watches as well (over a pregnant bitch) as he does over a woman.'

IV.
46.
O Maker of the material world, thou Holy One! If worshippers of Mazda want to have a bitch so covered that the offspring shall be one of a strong nature, what shall they do?

47.

AVESTA: Vendidad

Ahura Mazda answered: 'They shall dig a hole in the earth,
in the middle of the fold half a foot deep if the earth be hard,
half the height of a man if the earth be soft.
48.
'They shall first tie up [the bitch] there, far from children
and from the Fire, the son of Ahura Mazda, and they shall watch
by her until a dog comes there from anywhere; then another again,
and then a third again, each being kept apart from the former,
lest they should assail one another.
49.
'The bitch being thus covered by three dogs, grows big with
young, and the milk comes to her teats and she brings forth a
young one that is born from several dogs.'
50.
If a man smite a bitch who has been covered by three dogs,
and who has already milk, and who shall bring forth a young one
born from several dogs, what is the penalty that he shall pay?
51.
Ahura Mazda answered: 'Seven hundred stripes with the Aspahe-astra,
seven hundred stripes with the Sraosho-charana.'

FARGARD 16. Purity laws regarding menstruation

I.
1.
O Maker of the material world, thou Holy One! If there be
in the house of a worshipper of Mazda a woman who has the whites
or sees blood, what shall the worshippers of Mazda do?
2.
Ahura Mazda answered: 'They shall clear the way of the wood
there, both plants and trees; they shall strew dry dust on the
ground; and they shall isolate a half, or a third, or a fourth,

AVESTA: Vendidad

or a fifth part of the house, lest her look should fall upon the fire.'
3.
O Maker of the material world, thou Holy One! How far from the fire? How far from the water? How far from the consecrated bundles of Baresma? How far from the faithful?
4.
Ahura Mazda answered: 'Fifteen paces from the fire, fifteen paces from the water, fifteen paces from the consecrated bundles of Baresma, three paces from the faithful.'
5.
O Maker of the material world, thou Holy One! How far from her shall he stay, who brings food to a woman who has the whites or sees the blood?
6.
Ahura Mazda answered: 'Three paces from her shall he stay, who brings food to a woman who has the whites or sees the blood.'

In what kind of vessels shall he bring her bread? In what kind of vessels shall he bring her barley-drink?
'In vessels of brass, or of lead, or of any common metal.'
7.
How much bread shall he bring to her? How much barley-drink shall he bring?
'Two danares of dry bread, and one danare of liquor, lest she should get too weak.
'If a child has just touched her, they shall first wash his hands and then his body.

II.
8.
'If she still see blood after three nights have passed, she shall sit in the place of infirmity until four nights have passed.

'If she still see blood after four nights have passed, she shall

AVESTA: Vendidad

sit in the place of infirmity until five nights have passed.

9.
'If she still see blood after five nights have passed, she
shall sit in the place of infirmity until six nights have passed.

'If she still see blood after six nights have passed, she shall
sit in the place of infirmity until seven nights have passed.

10.
'If she still see blood after seven nights have passed, she
shall sit in the place of infirmity until eight nights have passed.

'If she still see blood after eight nights have passed, she shall
sit in the place of infirmity until nine nights have passed.

11.
'If she still see blood after nine nights have passed, this
is a work of the Daevas which they have performed for the worship
and glorification of the Daevas.
'The worshippers of Mazda shall clear the way of the wood there,
both plants and trees;

12.
'They shall dig three holes in the earth, and they shall wash
the woman with gomez by two of those holes and with water by the
third.
'They shall kill Khrafstras, to wit: two hundred corn-carrying
ants, if it be summer; two hundred of any other sort of the Khrafstras
made by Angra Mainyu, if it be winter.'

III.
13.
If a worshipper of Mazda shall suppress the issue of a woman
who has the whites or sees blood, what is the penalty that he
shall pay?
Ahura Mazda answered: 'He is a Peshotanu: two hundred stripes
with the Aspahe-astra, two hundred stripes with the Sraosho-charana.'
14.

AVESTA: Vendidad

O Maker of the material world, thou Holy One! If a man shall again and again lasciviously touch the body of a woman who has the whites or sees blood, so that the whites turn to the blood or the blood turns to the whites, what is the penalty that he shall pay?
15.
Ahura Mazda answered: 'For the first time he comes near unto her, for the first time he lies by her, thirty stripes with the Aspahe–astra, thirty stripes with the Sraosho–charana.
'For the second time he comes near unto her, for the second time he lies by her, fifty stripes with the Aspahe–astra, fifty stripes with the Sraosho–charana.
'For the third time he comes near unto her, for the third time he lies by her, seventy stripes with the Aspahe–astra, seventy stripes with the Sraosho–charana.'
16.
For the fourth time he comes near unto her, for the fourth time he lies by her, if he shall press the body under her clothes, if he shall go in between the unclean thighs, but without sexual intercourse, what is the penalty that he shall pay?
Ahura Mazda answered: 'Ninety stripes with the Aspahe–astra, ninety stripes with the Sraosho–charana.
17.
'Whosoever shall he in sexual intercourse with a woman who has the whites or sees blood does no better deed than if he should burn the corpse of his own son, born of his own body and dead of naeza, and drop its fat into the fire.
18.
'All wicked, embodiments of the Druj, are scorners of the judge: all scorners of the judge are rebels against the Sovereign: all rebels against the Sovereign are ungodly men; and all ungodly men are worthy of death.'

AVESTA: Vendidad

FARGARD 17. Hair and nails

I.
1.
Zarathushtra asked Ahura Mazda: 'O Ahura Mazda, most beneficent Spirit, Maker of the material world, thou Holy One! Which is the most deadly deed whereby a man offers up a sacrifice to the Daevas!'
2.
Ahura Mazda answered: 'It is when a man here below, combing his hair or shaving it off, or paring off his nails, drops them in a hole or in a crack.
3.
'Then by this transgression of the rites, Daevas are produced in the earth; by this transgression of the rites, those Khrafstras are produced in the earth which men call lice, and which eat up the corn in the corn-field and the clothes in the wardrobe.
4.
'Therefore, thou, O Zarathushtra! whenever here below thou shalt comb thy hair or shave it off, or pare off thy nails, thou shalt take them away ten paces from the faithful, twenty paces from the fire, thirty paces from the water, fifty paces from the consecrated bundles of Baresma.
5.
'Then thou shalt dig a hole, a disti [ten fingers] deep if the earth be hard, a vitasti [twelve fingers] deep if it be soft; thou shalt take the hair down there and thou shalt say aloud these victorious words: "For him, as a reward, Mazda made the plants grow up."
6.
'Thereupon thou shalt draw three furrows with a knife of metal around the hole, or six furrows or nine, and thou shall chant the Ahuna-Vairya three times, or six, or nine.

II.
7.
'For the nails, thou shalt dig a hole, out of the house, as
deep as the top joint of the little finger; thou shalt take the
nails down there and thou shalt say aloud these victorious words:
"The things that the pure proclaim through Asha and Vohu-mano."
8.
'Then thou shalt draw three furrows with a knife of metal
around the hole, or six furrows or nine, and thou shalt chant
the Ahuna-Vairya three times, or six, or nine.
9.
'And then: "O Asho-zushta bird! these nails I announce
and consecrate unto thee. May they be for thee so many spears
and knives, so many bows and falcon-winged arrows and so many
sling-stones against the Mazainya Daevas!"
10.
'If those nails have not been consecrated (to the bird), they
shall be in the hands of the Mazainya Daevas so many spears and
knives so many bows and falcon-winged arrows, and so many sling-stones
(against the Mazainya Daevas).
11.
'All wicked, embodiments of the Druj, are scorners of the
judge: all scorners of the judge are rebels against the Sovereign:
all rebels against the Sovereign are ungodly men; and all ungodly
men are worthy of death.'

FARGARD 18.

—

I.
1.
'There is many a one, O holy Zarathushtra!' said Ahura Mazda,

AVESTA: Vendidad

'Who wears a wrong Paitidana, and who has not girded his loins with the Religion; When such a man says, "I am an Athravan," he lies; do not call him an Athravan, O holy Zarathushtra!' thus said Ahura Mazda.

2.

'He holds a wrong Khrafstraghna in his hand and he has not girded his loins with the Religion; when he says, "I am an Athravan," he lies; do not call him an Athravan, O holy Zarathushtra! thus said Ahura Mazda.

3.

'He holds a wrong twig in his hand and he has not girded his loins with the Religion; when he says, "I am an Athravan," he lies; do not call him an Athravan, O holy Zarathushtra!' thus said Ahura Mazda.

4.

'He wields a wrong Astra mairya and he has not girded his loins with the Religion; when he says, "I am an Athravan," he lies; do not call him an Athravan, O holy Zarathushtra!' thus said Ahura Mazda.

5.

'He who sleeps on throughout the night, neither performing the Yasna nor chanting the hymns, worshipping neither by word nor by deed, neither learning nor teaching, with a longing for (everlasting) life, he lies when he says, "I am an Athravan," do not call him an Athravan, O holy Zarathushtra!' thus said Ahura Mazda.

6.

'Him thou shalt call an Athravan, O holy Zarathushtra! who throughout the night sits up and demands of the holy Wisdom, which makes man free from anxiety, and wide of heart, and easy of conscience at the head of the Chinwad bridge, and which makes him reach that world, that holy world, that excellent world of Paradise.

7.

'(Therefore) demand of me, thou upright one! of me, who am the Maker, the most beneficent of all beings, the best knowing, the most pleased in answering what is asked of me; demand of me,

AVESTA: Vendidad

that thou mayst be the better, that thou mayst be the happier.'
8.
Zarathushtra asked Ahura Mazda: 'O Maker of the material world, thou Holy One! What is it that brings in the unseen power of Death?'
9.
Ahura Mazda answered: 'It is the man that teaches a wrong Religion; it is the man who continues for three springs without wearing the sacred girdle, without chanting the Gathas, without worshipping the Good Waters.
10.
'And he who should set that man at liberty, when bound in prison, does no better deed than if he should cut a man's head off his neck.
11.
'For the blessing uttered by a wicked, ungodly Ashemaogha does not go past the mouth (of the blesser); the blessing of two Ashemaoghas does not go past the tongue; the blessing of three is nothing; the blessing of four turns to self-cursing.
12.
'Whosoever should give to a wicked, ungodly Ashemaogha either some Haoma prepared, or some Myazda consecrated with blessings, does no better deed than if he should lead a thousand horse against the boroughs of the worshippers of Mazda, and should slaughter the men thereof, and drive off the cattle as plunder.
13.
'Demand of me, thou upright one! of me, who am the Maker, the most beneficent of all beings, the best knowing, the most pleased in answering what is asked of me; demand of me, that thou mayst be the better, that thou mayst be the happier.'

II.
14.
Zarathushtra asked Ahura Mazda: 'Who is the Sraosha-varez of Sraosha? the holy, strong Sraosha, who is Obedience incarnate, a Sovereign with an astounding weapon.'

AVESTA: Vendidad

15.
Ahura Mazda answered: 'It is the bird named Parodars, which ill-speaking people call Kahrkatas, O holy Zarathushtra! the bird that lifts up his voice against the mighty Ushah:

16.
"'Arise, O men! recite the Ashem yad vahistem that smites down the Daevas. Lo! here is Bushyasta, the long-handed, coming upon you, who lulls to sleep again the whole living world, as soon as it has awoke: 'Sleep!' [she says,] 'O poor man! the time is not yet come.'"

17.
"'On the three excellent things be never intent, namely, good thoughts, good words, and good deeds; on the three abominable things be ever intent, namely, bad thoughts, bad words, and bad deeds."

18.
'On the first part of the night, Atar, the son of Ahura Mazda, calls the master of the house for help, saying:

19.
"'Up! arise, thou master of the house! put on thy girdle on thy clothes, wash thy hands, take wood, bring it unto me, and let me burn bright with the clean wood, carried by thy well-washed hands. Here comes Azi, made by the Daevas, who consumes me and wants to put me out of the world."

20.
'On the second part of the night, Atar, the son of Ahura Mazda, calls the husbandman for help, saying;

21.
"'Up! arise, thou husbandman! Put on thy girdle on thy clothes, wash thy hands, take wood, bring it unto me, and let me burn bright with the clean wood, carried by thy well-washed hands. Here comes Azi, made by the Daevas, who consumes me and wants to put me out of the world."

22.
'On the third part of the night, Atar, the son of Ahura Mazda, calls the holy Sraosha for help, saying: "Come thou, holy,

AVESTA: Vendidad

well-formed Sraosha, [then he brings unto me some clean wood with his well-washed hands.] Here comes Azi, made by the Daevas, who consumes me and wants to put me out of the world."

23.
'And then the holy Sraosha wakes up the bird named Parodars, which ill-speaking people call Kahrkatas, and the bird lifts up his voice against the mighty Ushah:

24.
"'Arise, O men! recite the Ashem yad vahistem [Ashem Vohu] and the Naismi daevo [the Creed, Y12]. Lo! here is Bushyasta, the long-handed, coming upon you, who lulls to sleep again the whole living world as soon as it has awoke: 'Sleep!' [she says,] 'O poor man! the time is not yet come.'"

25.
"'On the three excellent things be never intent, namely, good thoughts, good words, and good deeds; on the three abominable things be ever intent, namely, bad thoughts, bad words, and bad deeds."

26.
'And then bed-fellows address one another: "Rise up, here is the cock calling me up." Whichever of the two first gets up shall first enter Paradise: whichever of the two shall first, with well-washed hands, bring clean wood unto Atar, the son of Ahura Mazda, Atar, well pleased with him and not angry, and fed as it required, will thus bless him:

27.
"'May herds of oxen and sons accrue to thee: may thy mind be master of its vow, may thy soul be master of its vow, and mayst thou live on in the joy of thy soul all the nights of thy life."
'This is the blessing which Atar speaks unto him who brings him dry wood, well examined by the light of the day, well cleansed with godly intent.

28.
'And whosoever will kindly and piously present one of the faithful with a pair of these my Parodars birds, a male and a

AVESTA: Vendidad

female, O Spitama Zarathushtra! it is as though he had given a house with a hundred columns, a thousand beams, ten thousand large windows, ten thousand small windows.

29.
'And whosoever shall give meat to one of the faithful, as much of it as the body of this Parodars bird of mine, I, Ahura Mazda, need not interrogate him twice; he shall directly go to Paradise.'

III.

30.
The holy Sraosha, letting his club down upon her asked the Druj: 'O thou wretched, worthless Druj! Thou then, alone in the material world, dost bear offspring without any male coming unto thee?'

31.
The Druj demon answered: 'O holy, well-formed Sraosha! It is not so, nor do I, alone in the material world, bear offspring without any male coming unto me.

32.
'For there are four males of mine; and they make me conceive progeny as other males make their females conceive by their seed.'

33.
The holy Sraosha, letting his club down upon her, asked the Druj: 'O thou wretched, worthless Druj! Who is the first of those males of thine?'

34.
The Druj demon answered: 'O holy, well-formed Sraosha! He is the first of my males who, being entreated by one of the faithful, does not give him anything, be it ever so little, of the riches he has treasured up.

35.
'That man makes me conceive progeny as other males make their females conceive by their seed.'

36.

AVESTA: Vendidad

The holy Sraosha, letting his club down upon her, asked the
Druj: 'O thou wretched, worthless Druj! What is the thing that
can undo that?'
37.
The Druj demon answered: 'O holy, well-formed Sraosha! This
is the thing that undoes it, namely, when a man unasked, kindly
and piously, gives to one of the faithful something, be it ever
so little, of the riches he has treasured up.
38.
'He does thereby as thoroughly destroy the fruit of my womb
as a four-footed wolf does, who tears the child out of a mother's
womb.'
39.
The holy Sraosha, letting down his club upon her, asked the
Druj: 'O thou wretched, worthless Druj! Who is the second of those
males of thine?'
40.
The Druj demon answered: 'O holy, well-formed Sraosha! He
is the second of my males who, making water, lets it fall along
the upper forepart of his foot.
41.
'That man makes me conceive progeny as other males make their
females conceive by their seed.'
42.
The holy Sraosha, letting his club down upon her, asked the
Druj: 'O thou wretched, worthless Druj! What is the thing that
can undo that?'
43.
The Druj demon answered: 'O holy, wall-formed Sraosha! This
is the thing that undoes it, namely, when the man rising up and
stepping three steps further off, shall say three Ahuna-Vairya,
two humatanam, three hukhshathrotemam, and then chant the Ahuna-Vairya
and offer up one Yenhe hatam.
44.
'He does thereby as thoroughly destroy the fruit of my womb
as a four-footed wolf does, 'who tears the child out of a mother's

AVESTA: Vendidad

womb.'
45.

The holy Sraosha, letting his club down upon her, asked the Druj: 'O thou wretched, worthless Druj! Who is the third of those males of thine?'
46.

The Druj demon answered: 'O holy, well-formed Sraosha! He is the third of my males who during his sleep emits seed.
47.

'That man makes me conceive progeny as other males make their females conceive progeny by their seed.'
48.

The holy Sraosha, letting his club down upon her, asked the Druj: 'O thou wretched, worthless Druj! What is the thing that can undo that?'
49.

The Druj demon answered: 'O holy, well-formed Sraosha! this is the thing that undoes it, namely, if the man, when he has risen from sleep, shall say three Ahuna-Vairya, two humatanam, three hukhshathrotemam, and then chant the Ahuna-Vairya and offer up one Yenhe hatam.
50.

'He does thereby as thoroughly destroy the fruit of my womb as a four-footed wolf does who tears the child out of a mother's womb.'
51.

Then he shall speak unto Spenta Armaiti, saying: 'O Spenta Armaiti, this man do I deliver unto thee; this man deliver thou back unto me, against the happy day of resurrection; deliver him back as one who knows the Gathas, who knows the Yasna, and the revealed Law, a wise and clever man, who is Obedience incarnate.
52.

'Then thou shalt call his name "Fire-creature, Fire-seed, Fire-offspring, Fire-land," or any name wherein is the word Fire.'
53.

AVESTA: Vendidad

The holy Sraosha, letting his club down upon her, asked the Druj: 'O thou wretched, worthless Druj! Who is the fourth of those males of thine?'

54.
The Druj demon answered: 'O holy, well-formed Sraosha! This one is my fourth male who, either man or woman, being more than fifteen years of age, walks without wearing the sacred girdle and the sacred shirt.

55.
'At the fourth step we Daevas, at once, wither him even to the tongue and the marrow, and he goes thenceforth with power to destroy the world of Righteousness, and he destroys it like the Yatus and the Zandas.'

56.
The holy Sraosha, letting his club down upon her, asked the Druj: 'O thou wretched, worthless Druj, what is the thing that can undo that?'

57.
The Druj demon answered: 'O holy, well-formed Sraosha! There is no means of undoing it;

58.
'When a man or a woman, being more than fifteen years of age, walks without wearing the sacred girdle or the sacred shirt.

59.
'At the fourth step we Daevas, at once, wither him even to the tongue and the marrow, and he goes thenceforth with power to destroy the world of Righteousness, and he destroys it like the Yatus and the Zandas.'

IV.
60.
Demand of me, thou upright one! of me who am the Maker, the most beneficent of all beings, the best knowing, the most pleased in answering what is asked of me; demand of me that thou mayst be the better, that thou mayst be the happier.

AVESTA: Vendidad

61.
Zarathushtra asked Ahura Mazda: 'Who grieves thee with the sorest grief? Who pains thee with the sorest pain?'
62.
Ahura Mazda answered: 'It is the Jahi [courtesan], O Spitama Zarathushtra! who mixes in her the seed of the faithful and the unfaithful, of the worshippers of Mazda and the worshippers of the Daevas, of the wicked and the righteous.
63.
'Her look dries up one–third of the mighty floods that run from the mountains, O Zarathushtra; her look withers one–third of the beautiful, golden–hued, growing plants, O Zarathushtra;
64.
'Her look withers one–third of the strength of Spenta Armaiti; and her touch withers in the faithful one–third of his good thoughts, of his good words, of his good deeds, one–third of his strength, of his victorious power, and of his holiness.
65.
'Verily I say unto thee, O Spitama Zarathushtra! such creatures ought to be killed even more than gliding snakes, than howling wolves, than the wild she–wolf that falls upon the fold, or than the she–frog that falls upon the waters with her thousandfold brood.'

V.
66.
Demand of me, thou upright one! of me who am the Maker, the most beneficent of all beings, the best knowing, the most pleased in answering what is asked of me; demand of me that thou mayst be the better, that thou mayst be the happier.
67–68.
Zarathushtra asked Ahura Mazda: 'If a man shall come unto a woman who has the whites or sees blood, and he does so wittingly and knowingly, and she allows it willfully, wittingly, and knowingly, what is the atonement for it, what is the penalty that he shall

AVESTA: Vendidad

pay to atone for the deed they have done?'

69.
Ahura Mazda answered: 'If a man shall come unto a woman who has the whites or sees blood, and he does so wittingly and knowingly, and she allows it willfully, wittingly, and knowingly;

70.
'He shall slay a thousand head of small cattle; he shall godly and piously offer up to the fire the entrails thereof together with Zaothra-libations; he shall bring the shoulder bones to the Good Waters.

71.
'He shall godly and piously bring unto the fire a thousand loads of soft wood, of Urvasna, Vohu-gaona, Vohu-kereti, Hadha-naepata, or of any sweet-scented plant.

72.
'He shall tie and consecrate a thousand bundles of Baresma; he shall godly and piously offer up to the Good Waters a thousand Zaothra-libations, together with the Haoma and the milk, cleanly prepared and well strained, – cleanly prepared and well strained by a pious man, and mixed with the roots of the tree known as Hadha-naepata.

73.
'He shall kill a thousand snakes of those that go upon the belly, two thousand of the other kind; he shall kill a thousand land-frogs and two thousand water-frogs; he shall kill a thousand corn-carrying ants and two thousand of the other kind.

74.
'He shall throw thirty bridges over canals; he shall undergo a thousand stripes with the Aspahe-astra, a thousand stripes with the Sraosho-karana.

75.
'This is the atonement, this is the penalty that he shall pay to atone for the deed that he has done.

76.
'If he shall pay it, he makes himself a viaticum into the world of the holy ones; if he shall not pay it, he makes himself

a viaticum into the world of the wicked, into that world, made of darkness, the offspring of darkness, which is Darkness' self.'

FARGARD 19.

I.
1.
From the region of the north, from the regions of the north, forth rushed Angra Mainyu, the deadly, the Daeva of the Daevas. And thus spake the evil-doer Angra Mainyu, the deadly: 'Druj, rush down and kill him,' O holy Zarathushtra! The Druj came rushing along, the demon Buiti, who is deceiving, unseen death.
2.
Zarathushtra chanted aloud the Ahuna-Vairya: 'The will of the Lord is the law of righteousness. The gifts of Vohu-mano to the deeds done in this world for Mazda. He who relieves the poor makes Ahura king.'
He offered the sacrifice to the good waters of the good Daitya!
He recited the profession of the worshippers of Mazda!
The Druj dismayed, rushed away, the demon Buiti, who is deceiving, unseen death.
3.
And the Druj said unto Angra Mainyu: 'Thou, tormenter, Angra Mainyu! I see no way to kill Spitama Zarathushtra, so great is the glory of the holy Zarathushtra.'
Zarathushtra saw (all this) within his soul: 'The wicked, the evil-doing Daevas (thought he) take counsel together for my death.'

Ia.
4.
Up started Zarathushtra, forward went Zarathushtra, unabated

AVESTA: Vendidad

by Akem-mano, by the hardness of his malignant riddles; he went swinging stones in his hand, stones as big as a house, which he obtained from the Maker, Ahura Mazda, he the holy Zarathushtra.

'Whereat on this wide, round earth, whose ends lie afar, whereat dost thou swing (those stones), thou who standest by the upper bank of the river Dareja, in the mansion of Pourushaspa?'

5.
Thus Zarathushtra answered Angra Mainyu: 'O evil-doer, Angra Mainyu! I will smite the creation of the Daeva; I will smite the Nasu, a creature of the Daeva; I will smite the Pairika Knathaiti, till the victorious Saoshyant come up to life out of the lake Kasava, from the region of the dawn, from the regions of the dawn.'

6.
Again to him said the Maker of the evil world, Angra Mainyu: 'Do not destroy my creatures, O holy Zarathushtra! Thou art the son of Pourushaspa; by thy mother I was invoked. Renounce the good Religion of the worshippers of Mazda, and thou shalt gain such a boon as Vadhaghna gained, the ruler of the nations.'

7.
Spitama Zarathushtra said in answer: 'No! never will I renounce the good Religion of the worshippers of Mazda, either for body or life, though they should tear away the breath!'

8.
Again to him said the Maker of the evil world, Angra Mainyu: 'By whose Word wilt thou strike, by whose Word wilt thou repel, by whose weapon will the good creatures (strike and repel) my creation, who am Angra Mainyu?'

9.
Spitama Zarathushtra said in answer: 'The sacred mortar, the sacred cups, the Haoma, the Word taught by Mazda, these are my weapons, my best weapons! By this Word will I strike, by this Word will I repel, by this weapon will the good creatures (strike and repel thee), O evil-doer, Angra Mainyu! The Good Spirit made the creation; he made it in the boundless Time. The Amesha-Spentas made the creation, the good, the wise Sovereigns.'

AVESTA: Vendidad

10.
Zarathushtra chanted aloud the Ahuna–Vairya.
The holy Zarathushtra said aloud: 'This I ask thee: teach me the truth, O Lord! ...'

II.
11.
Zarathushtra asked Ahura Mazda: 'O Ahura Mazda, most beneficent spirit, Maker of the material world, thou Holy One! [he was sitting by the upper bank of the Dareja, before Ahura Mazda, before the good Vohu–mana, before Asha Vahista, Khshathra Vairya, and Spenta Armaiti;]
12.
'How shall I free the world from that Druj, from that evil–doer, Angra Mainyu? How shall I drive away direct defilement? How indirect defilement? How shall I drive the Nasu from the house of the worshippers of Mazda? How shall I cleanse the faithful man? How shall I cleanse the faithful woman?'
13.
Ahura Mazda answered: 'Invoke, O Zarathushtra! the good Religion of Mazda.
'Invoke, O Zarathushtra! though thou see them not, the Amesha–Spentas who rule over the seven Karshvares of the earth.
'Invoke, O Zarathushtra! the sovereign Heaven, the boundless Time, and Vayu, whose action is most high.
'Invoke, O Zarathushtra! the powerful Wind, made by Mazda; and Spenta [Armaiti], the fair daughter of Ahura Mazda.
14.
'Invoke, O Zarathushtra! my Fravashi, who am Ahura Mazda, the greatest, the best, the fairest of all beings, the most solid, the most intelligent, the best shapen, the highest in holiness, and whose soul is the holy Word!
'Invoke, O Zarathushtra! this creation of mine, who am Ahura Mazda.'
15.
Zarathushtra imitated my words from me, (and said): 'I invoke

AVESTA: Vendidad

the holy creation of Ahura Mazda.
'I invoke Mithra, the lord of the rolling countryside, a god armed with beautiful weapons, with the most glorious of all weapons, with the most victorious of all weapons.
'I invoke the holy, well-formed Sraosha', who wields a club in his hand, to bear upon the heads of the fiends'.
16.
'I invoke the most glorious Holy Word.
'I invoke the sovereign Heaven, the boundless Time, and Vayu, whose action is most high.
'I invoke the mighty Wind, made by Mazda, and Spenta (Armaiti), the fair daughter of Ahura Mazda.
'I invoke the good Religion of Mazda, the fiend-destroying Law of Zarathushtra.'

III.
17.
Zarathushtra asked Ahura Mazda: 'O Maker of the good world, Ahura Mazda! With what manner of sacrifice shall I worship, with what manner of sacrifice shall I make people worship this creation of Ahura Mazda?'
18.
Ahura Mazda answered: 'Go, O Spitama Zarathushtra! towards the high-growing trees, and before one of them that is beautiful, high-growing, and mighty, say thou these words: "Hail to thee! O good, holy tree, made by Mazda! Ashem vohu!"
19.
'[The priest] shall cut off a twig of Baresma, long as an aesha, thick as a yava. The faithful one, holding it in his left hand, shall keep his eyes upon it without ceasing, whilst he is offering up to Ahura Mazda and to the Amesha-Spentas, the high and beautiful golden Haomas, and Good Thought and the good Rata, made by Mazda, holy and excellent.'

AVESTA: Vendidad

IV.

20.

Zarathushtra asked Ahura Mazda: 'O thou, all-knowing Ahura Mazda! thou art never asleep, never intoxicated, thou Ahura Mazda! Vohu-mano gets directly defiled: Vohu-mano gets indirectly defiled; the Daevas defile him from the bodies smitten by the Daevas: let Vohu-mano be made clean.'

21.

Ahura Mazda answered: 'Thou shalt take some gomez from a bull ungelded and such as the law requires it. Thou shalt take the man who is to be cleansed to the field made by Ahura, and the man that is to cleanse him shall draw the furrows.

22.

'He shall recite a hundred Ashem vohu: "Holiness is the best of all good: it is also happiness. Happy the man who is holy with perfect holiness!"

'He shall chant two hundred Ahuna-Vairya: "The will of the Lord is the law of righteousness. The gifts of Vohu-mano to the deeds done in this world for Mazda! He who relieves the poor makes Ahura king."

'He shall wash himself four times with the gomez from the ox, and twice with the water made by Mazda.

23.

'Thus Vohu-mano shall be made clean, and clean shall be the man. The man shall take up Vohu-mano with the left arm and the right, with the right arm and the left: and thou shalt lay down Vohu-mano under the mighty light of the heavens by the light of the stars made by the gods, until nine nights have passed away.

24.

'When nine nights have passed away, thou shalt bring libations unto the fire, thou shalt bring hard wood unto the fire, thou shalt bring incense of Vohu-gaona unto the fire, and thou shalt perfume Vohu-mano therewith.

25.

'Thus shall Vohu-mano be made clean, and clean shall be the man. He shall take up Vohu-mano with the right arm and the left,

AVESTA: Vendidad

with the left arm and the right, and Vohu-mano shall say aloud: "Glory be to Ahura Mazda! Glory be to the Amesha-Spentas! Glory be to all the other holy beings."'

V.

26.
Zarathushtra asked Ahura Mazda: 'O thou all-knowing Ahura Mazda: Should I urge upon the godly man, should I urge upon the godly woman, should I urge upon the wicked Daeva-worshipper who lives in sin, to give the earth made by Ahura, the water that runs, the corn that grows, and all the rest of their wealth?'

Ahura Mazda answered: 'Thou shouldst, O holy Zarathushtra.'

27.
O Maker of the material world, thou Holy One! Where are the rewards given? Where does the rewarding take place? Where is the rewarding fulfilled? Whereto do men come to take the reward that, during their life in the material world, they have won for their souls?

28.
Ahura Mazda answered: 'When the man is dead, when his time is over, then the wicked, evil-doing Daevas cut off his eyesight. On the third night, when the dawn appears and brightens up, when Mithra, the god with beautiful weapons, reaches the all-happy mountains, and the sun is rising:

29.
'Then the fiend, named Vizaresha, O Spitama Zarathushtra, carries off in bonds the souls of the wicked Daeva-worshippers who live in sin. The soul enters the way made by Time, and open both to the wicked and to the righteous. At the head of the Chinwad bridge, the holy bridge made by Mazda, they ask for their spirits and souls the reward for the worldly goods which they gave away here below.

30.
'Then comes the beautiful, well-shapen, strong and well-formed

AVESTA: Vendidad

maid, with the dogs at her sides, one who can distinguish, who
has many children, happy, and of high understanding.
'She makes the soul of the righteous one go up above the Hara-berezaiti;
above the Chinwad bridge she places it in the presence of the
heavenly gods themselves.

31.
'Up rises Vohu-mano from his golden seat; Vohu-mano exclaims:
"How hast thou come to us, thou Holy One, from that decaying
world into this undecaying one?"

32.
'Gladly pass the souls of the righteous to the golden seat
of Ahura Mazda, to the golden seat of the Amesha-Spentas, to the
Garo-nmanem, the abode of Ahura Mazda, the abode of the Amesha-Spentas,
the abode of all the other holy beings.

33.
'As to the godly man that has been cleansed, the wicked evil-doing
Daevas tremble at the perfume of his soul after death, as doth
a sheep on which a wolf is pouncing.

34.
'The souls of the righteous are gathered together there: Nairyo-sangha
is with them; a messenger of Ahura Mazda is Nairyo-sangha.

IIa.
'Invoke, O Zarathushtra! this very creation of Ahura Mazda.'
35.
Zarathushtra imitated those words of mine: 'I invoke the holy
world, made by Ahura Mazda.
'I invoke the earth made by Ahura, the water made by Mazda, the
holy trees.
'I invoke the sea Vouru-kasha.
'I invoke the beautiful Heaven.
'I invoke the endless and sovereign Light.'
36.
'I invoke the bright, blissful Paradise of the Holy Ones.

AVESTA: Vendidad

'I invoke the Garo-nmanem, the abode of Ahura Mazda, the abode of the Amesha-Spentas, the abode of all the other holy beings.

'I invoke the sovereign Place of Eternal Weal, and the Chinwad bridge made by Mazda.

37.
'I invoke the good Saoka, who has the good eye.
'I invoke the whole creation of weal.
'I invoke the mighty Fravashis of the righteous.
'I invoke Verethraghna, made by Ahura, who wears the Glory made by Mazda.
'I invoke Tishtrya, the bright and glorious star, in the shape of a golden-horned bull.

38.
'I invoke the holy, beneficent Gathas, who rule over the Ratus:

'I invoke the Ahunavaiti Gatha;
'I invoke the Ushtavaiti Gatha;
'I invoke the Spenta-mainyu Gatha;
'I invoke the Vohu-khshathra Gatha;
'I invoke the Vahishtoishti Gatha.

39.
'I invoke the Karshvares of Arzahe and Savahe;
'I invoke the Karshvares of Fradadhafshu and Vidadhafshu;
'I invoke the Karshvares of Vourubaresti and Vouruzaresti;
'I invoke the bright Hvaniratha;
'I invoke the bright, glorious Haetumant;
'I invoke the good Ashi;
['I invoke the good Chisti;]
'I invoke the most pure Chista;
'I invoke the Glory of the Aryan regions;
'I invoke the Glory of the bright Yima, the good shepherd.

40.
'Let him be worshipped with sacrifice, let him be gladdened, gratified, and satisfied, the holy Sraosha, the well-formed, victorious, holy Sraosha.

AVESTA: Vendidad

'Bring libations unto the Fire, bring hard wood unto the Fire, bring incense of Vohu-gaona unto the Fire.

'Offer up the sacrifice to the Vazishta fire, which smites the fiend Spengaghra: bring unto it the cooked meat and full overflowing libations.

41.

'Offer up the sacrifice to the holy Sraosha, that the holy Sraosha may smite down the fiend Kunda, who is drunken without drinking, and throws down into the Hell of the Druj the wicked Daeva-worshippers, who live in sin.

[42.

'I invoke the Kara fish, who lives beneath waters in the bottom of the deep lakes.

'I invoke the ancient and sovereign Merezu, the most warlike of the creatures of the two Spirits.

'I invoke the seven bright Sru ...'

VI.

43.

'They cried about, their minds wavered to and fro, Angra Mainyu the deadly, the Daeva of the Daevas; Indra the Daeva, Sauru the Daeva, Naunghaithya the Daeva, Taurvi and Zairi; Aeshma of the murderous spear; Akatasha the Daeva; Winter, made by the Daevas; the deceiving, unseen Death; Zaurva, baneful to the fathers; Buiti the Daeva; Driwi the Daeva; Daiwi the Daeva; Kasvi the Daeva; Paitisha the most Daeva-like amongst the Daevas.]

44.

'And the evil-doing Daeva, Angra Mainyu, the deadly, said: "What! let the wicked, evil-doing Daevas gather together at the head of Arezura!"

45.

'They rush away shouting, the wicked, evil-doing Daevas; they run away shouting, the wicked, evil-doing Daevas; they run away casting the Evil Eye, the wicked, evil-doing Daevas: "Let us gather together at the head of Arezura!

AVESTA: Vendidad

46.

'"For he is just born the holy Zarathushtra, in the house of Pourushaspa. How can we procure his death? He is the weapon that fells the fiends: he is a counter-fiend to the fiends; he is a Druj to the Druj. Vanished are the Daeva-worshippers, the Nasu made by the Daeva, the false-speaking Lie!"

47.

'They rush away shouting, the wicked, evil-doing Daevas, into the depths of the dark, raging world of hell.

'Ashem vohu: Holiness is the best of all good.'

FARGARD 20. Thrita, the First Healer.

1.

Zarathushtra asked Ahura Mazda: 'Ahura Mazda, most beneficent Spirit, Maker of the material world, thou Holy One! Who was he who first of the healers, of the wise, the happy, the wealthy, the glorious, the strong, the Paradhatas, drove back sickness to sickness, drove back death to death; and first turned away the point of the sword and the fire of fever from the bodies of mortals?'

2.

Ahura Mazda answered: 'Thrita it was who first of the healers, of the wise, the happy, the wealthy, the glorious, the strong, the Paradhatas, drove back sickness to sickness, drove back death to death, and first turned away the point of the sword and the fire of fever from the bodies of mortals.

3.

'He asked for a source of remedies; he obtained it from Khshathra-Vairya, to withstand sickness and to withstand death; to withstand pain and to withstand fever; to withstand Sarana and to withstand Sarastya; to withstand Azana and to withstand Azahva; to withstand Kurugha

AVESTA: Vendidad

and. to withstand Azivaka; to withstand Duruka and to 'withstand Astairya; to withstand the evil eye, rottenness, and infection which Angra Mainyu had created against the bodies of mortals.
4.
'And I Ahura Mazda brought down the healing plants that, by many hundreds, by many thousands, by many myriads, grow up all around the one Gaokerena.
5.
'All this do we achieve; all this do we order; all these prayers do we utter, for the benefit of the bodies of mortals;
6.
'To withstand sickness and to withstand death; to withstand pain and to withstand fever; to withstand Sarana and to withstand Sarastya; to withstand Azana and to withstand Azahva; to withstand Kurugha and to withstand Azivaka; to withstand Duruka and to withstand Astairya; to withstand the evil eye, rottenness, and infection which Angra Mainyu has created against the bodies of mortals.
7.
'To thee, O Sickness, I say avaunt! to thee, O Death, I say avaunt! to thee, O Pain, I say avaunt! to thee, O Fever, I say avaunt! to thee, O Evil Eye, I say avaunt! to thee, O Sarana, I say avaunt! and to thee, O Sarastya, I say avaunt! to thee, O Azana, I say avaunt! and to thee, O Azahva, I say avaunt! to thee, O Kurugha, I say avaunt! and to thee, O Azivaka, I say avaunt! to thee, O Duruka, I say avaunt! and to thee, O Astairya, I say avaunt!
8.
'Give us, O Ahura, that powerful sovereignty, by the strength of which we may smite down the Druj! By its might may we smite the Druj!
9.
'I drive away Ishire and I drive away Aghuire; I drive away Aghra and I drive away Ughra; I drive away sickness and I drive away death; I drive away pain and I drive away fever; I drive away Sarana and I drive away Sarastya; I drive away Azana and I drive away Azahva; I drive away Kurugha and I drive away Azivaka;

AVESTA: Vendidad

I drive away Duruka and I drive away Astairya; I drive away the
evil eye, rottenness, and infection which Angra Mainyu has created
against the bodies of mortals.
10.
'I drive away all manner of sickness and death, all the Yatus
and Pairikas, and all the wicked Jainis.
11.
'A Airyama ishyo. May the vow-fulfilling Airyaman come here,
for the men and women of Zarathushtra to rejoice, for Vohu-mano
to rejoice; with the desirable reward that Religion deserves.
I solicit for holiness that boon that is vouchsafed by Ahura!
12.
'May the vow-fulfilling Airyaman smite all manner of sickness
and death, all the Yatus and Pairikas, and all the wicked Jainis.'
[13.
Yatha ahu vairyo:– The will of the Lord is the law of righteousness.

The gifts of Vohu-mano to the deeds done in this world for Mazda.
He who relieves the poor makes Ahura king.
Kem-na Mazda:– What protector hast thou given unto me, O Mazda!
while the hate of the wicked encompasses me? Whom but thy Atar
and Vohu-mano, through whose work I keep on the world of Righteousness?
Reveal therefore to me thy Religion as thy rule!
Ke verethrem-ja:– Who is the victorious who will protect thy teaching?
Make it clear that I am the guide for both worlds. May Sraosha
come with Vohu-mano and help whomsoever thou pleasest, O Mazda!

Keep us from our hater, O Mazda and Armaiti Spenta! Perish, O
fiendish Druj! Perish, O brood of the fiend! Perish, O world of
the fiend! Perish away, O Druj! Perish away to the regions of
the north, never more to give unto death the living world of Righteousness!]

AVESTA: Vendidad

FARGARD 21.

I.
1.
Hail, bounteous bull! Hail to thee, beneficent bull! Hail to thee, who makest increase! Hail to thee, who makest growth! Hail to thee, who dost bestow his part upon the righteous faithful, and wilt bestow it on the faithful yet unborn! Hail to thee, whom the Jahi kills, and the ungodly Ashemaogha, and the wicked tyrant.

II.
2.
'Come, come on, O clouds, from up above, down on the earth, by thousands of drops, by myriads of drops:' thus say, O holy Zarathushtra! 'to destroy sickness, to destroy death, to destroy the sickness that kills, to destroy death that kills, to destroy Gadha and Apagadha.
3.
'If death come after noon, may healing come at eve!
'If death come at eve, may healing come at night!
'If death come at night, may healing come at dawn!
'And showers shower down new water, new earth, new plants, new healing powers, and new healing.

IIIa.
4.
'As the sea Vouru-kasha is the gathering place of the waters, rising up and going down, up the aerial way and down the earth, down the earth and up the aerial way: thus rise up and roll along! thou in whose rising and growing Ahura Mazda made the aerial way.
5.

AVESTA: Vendidad

'Up! rise up and roll along! thou swift-horsed Sun, above
Hara Berezaiti, and produce light for the world (and mayst thou
[O man!] rise up there, if thou art to abide in Garo-nmanem)4,
along the path made by Mazda, along the way made by the gods,
the watery way they opened.
6.
'And the Holy Word shall keep away the evil: Of thee [O child!]
I will cleanse the birth and growth; of thee [O woman!] I will
make the body and the strength pure; I make thee rich in children
and rich in milk;
7.
'Rich in seed, in milk, in fat, in marrow, and in offspring.
I shall bring to thee a thousand pure springs, running towards
the pastures that give food to the child.

IIIb.
8.
'As the sea Vouru-kasha is the gathering place of the waters,
rising up and going down, up the aerial way and down the earth,
down the earth and up the aerial way:
'Thus rise up and roll along! thou in whose rising and growing
Ahura Mazda made the earth.
9.
'Up! rise up, thou Moon, that dost keep in thee the seed of
the bull;
'Rise up above Hara Berezaiti, and produce light for the world
(and mayst thou [O man!] rise up there, if thou art to abide in
Garo-nmanem), along the path made by Mazda, along the way made
by the gods, the watery way they opened.
10.
'And the Holy Word shall keep away the evil: Of thee [O child!]
I will cleanse the birth and growth; of thee [O woman!] I will
make the body and the strength pure; I make thee rich in children
and rich in milk;
11.

AVESTA: Vendidad

'Rich in seed, in milk, in fat, in marrow, and in offspring.
I shall bring to thee a thousand pure springs, running towards
the pastures that give food to the child.

IIIc.
12.
'As the sea Vouru-kasha is the gathering place of the waters,
rising up and going down, up the aerial way and down the earth,
down the earth and up the aerial way:
'Thus rise up and roll along! thou in whose rising and growing
Ahura Mazda made everything that grows.
13.
'Up! rise up, ye deep Stars, that have in you the seed of
waters;
'Rise up above Hara Berezaiti and produce light for the world
(and mayst thou [O man!] rise up there, if thou art to abide in
Gara-nmanem), along the path made by Mazda. along the way made
by the gods, the watery way they opened.
14.
'And the Holy Word shall keep away the evil: Of thee [O child!]
I will cleanse the birth and growth; of thee [O woman!] I will
make the body and the strength pure; I make thee rich in children
and rich in milk;
15.
'Rich in seed, in milk, in fat, in marrow, and in offspring.
I shall bring to thee a thousand pure springs, running towards
the pastures that will give food to the child.
16.
'As the sea Vouru-kasha is the gathering place of the waters,
rising up and going down, up the aerial way and down the earth,
down the earth and up the aerial way:
'Thus rise up and roll along! ye in whose rising and growing Ahura
Mazda made everything that rises.
17.
'In your rising away will the Kahvuzi fly and cry, away will

AVESTA: Vendidad

the Ayehi fly and cry, away will the Jahi who follows the Yatu, fly and cry.

IV.
[18.
'I drive away Ishire and I drive away Aghuire; I drive away Aghra and I drive away Ughra; I drive away sickness and I drive away death; I drive away pain and I drive away fever; I drive away Sarana and I drive away Sarastya. I drive away Azana and I drive away Azahva; I drive away Kurugha and I drive away Azhivaka; l drive away Duruka and I drive away Astairya; I drive away the evil eye, rottenness, and infection which Angra Mainyu has created against the bodies of mortals.
19.
'I drive away all manner of sickness and death, all the Yatus and Pairikas, and all the wicked Jainis.
20.
'A Airyama ishyo:– May the vow-fulfilling Airyaman come here, for the men and women of Zarathushtra to rejoice, for Vohu-mano to rejoice; with the desirable reward that Religion deserves. I solicit for holiness that boon that is vouchsafed by Ahura!
21.
'May the vow-fulfilling Airyaman smite all manner of sickness and death, all the Yatus and Pairikas, and all the wicked Jainis.
22.
'Yatha ahu vairyo:– The will of the Lord is the law of righteousness!

'Kem-na Mazda:– What protector hast thou given unto me ... ?
'Ke verethrem-ja:– Who is the victorious who will protect thy teaching ... ?
23.
'Keep us from our hater, O Mazda and Armaiti Spenta! Perish, O fiendish Druj! Perish, O brood of the fiend! Perish, O world of the fiend! Perish away, O Druj! Perish away to the regions of the north, never more to give unto death the living world of

Righteousness!]

FARGARD 22. Angra Mainyu creates 99,999 diseases; Ahura Mazda counters with the Holy Manthra and with Airyaman

I.
1.
Ahura Mazda spake unto Spitama Zarathushtra, saying: 'I, Ahura Mazda, the Maker of all good things, when I made this mansion, the beautiful, the shining, seen afar (there may I go up, there may I arrive!)
2.
'Then the ruffian looked at me; the ruffian Angra Mainyu, the deadly, wrought against me nine diseases, and ninety, and nine hundred, and nine thousand, and nine times ten thousand diseases. So mayst thou heal me, thou most glorious Mathra Spenta!
3.
'Unto thee will I give in return a thousand fleet, swift-running steeds; I offer thee up a sacrifice, O good Saoka, made by Mazda and holy.
'Unto thee will I give in return a thousand fleet, high-humped camels; I offer thee up a sacrifice, O good Saoka, made by Mazda and holy.
4.
'Unto thee will I give in return a thousand brown oxen that do not push; I offer thee up a sacrifice, O good Saoka, made by Mazda and holy.
'Unto thee will I give in return a thousand females big with young, of all species of small cattle; I offer thee up a sacrifice, O good Saoka, made by Mazda and holy.
5.

AVESTA: Vendidad

'And I will bless thee with the fair blessing-spell of the righteous, the friendly blessing-spell of the righteous, that makes the empty swell to fullness and the full to overflowing, that comes to help him who was sickening, and makes the sick man sound again.

6.

'Mathra Spenta, the all-glorious, replied unto me: "How shall I heal thee? How shall I drive away from thee those nine diseases, and those ninety, those nine hundred, those nine thousand, and those nine times ten thousand diseases?"'

II.
7.
The Maker Ahura Mazda called for Nairyo-sangha: Go thou, Nairyo-sangha, the herald, and drive towards the mansion of Airyaman, and speak thus unto him:

8.
Thus speaks Ahura Mazda, the Holy One, unto thee:
'I, Ahura Mazda, the Maker of all good things, when I made this mansion, the beautiful, the shining, seen afar (there may I ascend, there may I arrive!)

9.
'Then the ruffian looked at me; the ruffian Angra Mainyu, the deadly, wrought against me nine diseases, and ninety, and nine hundred, and nine thousand, and nine times ten thousand diseases. So mayst thou heal me, O Airyaman, the vow-fulfiller!

10.
'Unto thee will I give in return a thousand fleet, swift-running steeds; I offer thee up a sacrifice, O good Saoka, made by Mazda and holy,

'Unto thee will I give in return a thousand fleet, high-humped camels; I offer thee up a sacrifice, O good Saoka, made by Mazda and holy,

11.
'Unto thee will I give in return a thousand brown oxen that

AVESTA: Vendidad

do not push; I offer thee up a sacrifice, O good Saoka, made by
Mazda and holy.
'Unto thee will I give in return a thousand females big with young,
of all species of small cattle. I offer thee up a sacrifice, O
good Saoka, made by Mazda and holy.
12.
'And I will bless thee with the fair blessing-spell of the
righteous, the friendly blessing-spell of the righteous, that
make, the empty swell to fullness and the full to overflowing,
that comes to help him who was sickening, and makes the sick man
sound again.'

III.
13.
In obedience to Ahura's words he went, Nairyo-sangha, the
herald; he drove towards the mansion of Airyaman, he spake unto
Airyaman, saying:
14.
Thus speaks Ahura Mazda, the Holy One, unto thee: 'I, Ahura
Mazda, the Maker of all good things, when I made this mansion,
the beautiful, the shining, seen afar (there may I go up, there
may I arrive!)
15.
'Then the ruffian looked at me; the ruffian Angra Mainyu,
the deadly, wrought against me nine diseases, and ninety, and
nine hundred, and nine thousand, and nine times ten thousand diseases.
So mayst thou heal me, O Airyaman, the vow-fulfiller!
16.
'Unto thee will I give in return a thousand fleet, swift-running
steeds ; I offer thee up a sacrifice, O good Saoka, made by Mazda
and holy.
'Unto thee will I give in return a thousand fleet, high-humped
camels; I offer thee up a sacrifice, O good Saoka, made by Mazda
and holy.
17.

AVESTA: Vendidad

'Unto thee will I give in return a thousand brown oxen that
do not push; I offer thee up a sacrifice, O good Saoka, made by
Mazda and holy.
'Unto thee will I give in return a thousand females, big with
young, of all species of small cattle; I offer thee up a sacrifice,
O good Saoka, made by Mazda and holy.
18.
'And I will bless thee with the fair blessing-spell of the
righteous, the friendly blessing-spell of the righteous, that
makes the empty swell to fullness and the full to overflowing,
that comes to help him who was sickening, and makes the sick man
sound again.'

IV.
19.
Quickly was it done, nor was it long, eagerly set off the
vow-fulfilling Airyaman, towards the mountain of the holy Questions,
towards the forest of the holy Questions.
20.
Nine kinds of stallions brought he with him, the vow-fulfilling
Airyaman.
Nine hinds of camels brought he with him, the vow-fulfilling Airyaman.

Nine kinds of bulls brought he with him, the vow-fulfilling Airyaman.

Nine kinds of small cattle brought he with him, the vow-fulfilling
Airyaman.
He brought with him the nine twigs; he drew along nine furrows.
[21.
'I drive away Ishire and I drive away Aghuire; I drive away
Aghra and I drive away Ughra; I drive away sickness and I drive
away death; I drive away pain and I drive away fever; I drive
away Sarana and I drive away Sarastya; I drive away Azhana and
I drive away Azhahva; I drive away Kurugha and I drive away Azhivaka;
I drive away Duruka and I drive away Astairya. I drive away the

AVESTA: Vendidad

evil eye, rottenness, and infection which Angra Mainyu has created against the bodies of mortals.

22.

'I drive away all manner of sickness and death, all the Yatus and Pairikas, and all the wicked Jainis.

23.

'May the vow-fulfilling Airyaman come here, for the men and women of Zarathushtra to rejoice, for Vohu-mano to rejoice; with the desirable reward that Religion deserves. I solicit for holiness that boon that is vouchsafed by Ahura.

24.

'May the vow-fulfilling Airyaman smite all manner of sickness and death, all the Yatus and Pairikas, and all the wicked Jainis.

25.

'Yatha ahu vairyo:- The will of the Lord is the law of righteousness. The gifts of Vohu-mano to the deeds done in this world for Mazda. He who relieves the poor makes Ahura king.

'Kem-na Mazda:- What protector hast thou given unto me O Mazda! while the hate of the wicked encompasses me? Whom but thy Atar and Vohu-mano, through whose work I keep on the world of righteousness? Reveal therefore to me thy Religion as thy rule!

'Ke verethrem-ja:- Who is the victorious who will protect thy teaching? Make it clear that I am the guide for both worlds. May Sraosha come with Vohu-mano and help whomsoever thou pleasest, O Mazda!

'Keep us from our hater, O Mazda and Armaiti Spenta! Perish, O fiendish Druj! Perish, O brood of the fiend! Perish, O world of the fiend! Perish away, O Druj! Perish away to the regions of the north, never more to give unto death the living world of Righteousness!']

Printed in the United States
43152LVS00004B/11